About the Author

Born a 'Pads-Brat' in West Germany, David Ayre is the son of a British soldier and German mother. Having moved to Newcastle Upon Tyne in 1979, this is where he found his loves for writing and watching his beloved Newcastle United.

In his family tradition, he joined the British Army in 1993. David served many years working in various locations including back in Germany and Bosnia Herzegovina.

After leaving the forces, he married his partner from East Yorkshire having met her in Germany whilst serving abroad.

Now, married to that Yorkshire lass they have two children and have lived in East Yorkshire for over twenty years.

Pegasus Rising

David Ayre

Pegasus Rising

Olympia Publishers
London

www.olympiapublishers.com
OLYMPIA PAPERBACK EDITION

A CIP catalogue record for this title is available from the British
Library.

ISBN: 978-1-80074-202-4

First Published in 2024

Olympia Publishers
Tallis House
2 Tallis Street
London
EC4Y 0AB

Printed in Great Britain

Dedication

This work is dedicated to my wife Alison and our boys James and Jack. Thank you for being my everything.

PROLOGUE

On the 30th January 1972, British Paratroopers reportedly opened fire on Northern Irish protesters in the Bogside area of Derry, Northern Ireland, during a large, heated protest. That day, known forever more as *Bloody Sunday*, saw the deaths of fourteen civilian protestors. The ensuing investigation heard claims that the British Army opened fire first. There were counter-claims that protesters carried nail-bombs and that the Irish Republican Army (I.R.A) opened fire on their own countrymen and British forces first, with an aim of escalating the troubles. But what was clear, was that fourteen people were dead. Whether by British Army fire, or by I.R.A. fire. This then led to years of further bloodshed, mainly carried out by the I.R.A. using a variety of methods which included car-bombs, shootings, executions and arson carried out on both Irish and English soil.

Between the years of 1969 and 1997, the I.R.A had claimed the lives of six hundred and fifty-six British troops and two hundred and seventy-two R.U.C. (Royal Ulster Constabulary) officers. In the same time period, two hundred and ninety-three I.R.A. members were killed and over ten thousand jailed on terrorist related charges.

In 2007, the British Prime Minister, Tony Blair, held a secret meeting with Sinn Fein members, Gerry Adams and Martin McGuiness, at No.10 Downing Street, which resulted in the declaration, by Tony Blair to give two hundred and twenty-eight on-the-run members of the I.R.A. complete immunity from prosecution of previous atrocities. Of those two hundred and twenty-eight, one hundred and eighty-seven were given letters of comfort – physical pieces of paper granting them complete immunity from prosecution of past crimes. Tony Blair also campaigned to have I.R.A. members already imprisoned, released as part of an agreement known as 'The Good Friday' agreement. However, this request was thrown out of the Commons, not only by Britain's main political parties but also, oddly enough, by Sinn Fein themselves. Sinn Fein wanted to see British soldiers punished for their part in Bloody Sunday. If Sinn Fein had agreed to have their own members released and pardoned, then British soldiers too could not be held to account.

These letters of comfort were signed by major Irish heads of state and civil servants whose authority could only have come from the Prime Minister himself, Tony Blair.

CHAPTER ONE
DAWNING OF A NEW DAY

London, Great Britain. 18th March.

It was early morning. The sun was rising over a chilly and crisp London. Small, wispy clouds strayed randomly over a glorious orange and light blue skyline. All of London's well-known buildings were silhouetted against the dawning of a new morning sun. Queen Elizabeth Tower, The Shard, The Gherkin and The London Eye. The sun was rising on an important morning in Britain's history.

Milk deliveries were well under way, as was the mail. Pigeons fresh from a night's sleep flew circles in flocks over the city. The time was about five a.m. and the city was beginning to wake up for another busy day. There were young men and women out on their morning runs, adorned in high-vis vests and shorts with headphones, breath visible with every step in the chill of the early morning. Street sweeping vehicles collected rubbish from the edges of the roads. There was the odd cyclist making an early start to get to the office, and London taxis started to line up at the usual busy places such as Waterloo Station and Kings Cross for another busy day of commuting.

No. 10 Downing Street, London. 18th March - 06:29.

In a darkened bedroom, a couple slept soundly tucked up in bed. Only the occasional grunt could be heard. The first rays

11

of sunshine had just begun to creep through the gaps around the edges of the curtains. The LED clock on the bedside table had just flipped to 06:30 and the radio switched on. The early morning B.B.C. news headlines were being read out from the radio, talking about the Prime Minister and how she must face the Members of Parliament today to debate the trial of an ex-British army paratrooper found guilty of murder in Northern Ireland over four decades before. After a few moments, a hand reached out from underneath the covers of the bed and, as if imitating a spider walking, searched for the source of the sound. Eventually finding its goal, the hand slammed the buttons on the top of the alarm clock with a flat palm a number of times, as if trying to hit all of the buttons at once, hoping to hit any button to stop the noise. The radio stopped. There was silence for a few seconds as the hand slid slowly back beneath the covers before a man's voice came from the opposite side of the bed.

"Come on Patricia. Don't go back to sleep!"

A woman's voice replied with a tired, "Humm mm," in acknowledgement yet disagreement. A few more seconds passed in silence.

Again the man spoke, this time with a little more authority in his voice. "Patricia!" This time there was movement.

"Okay, okay," she said, slowly starting to move, trying to untangle herself from the pile of bedding. "Why do you get to stay in bed? It's not fair!" she said.

The man chuckled. "Because I'm not the Prime Minister!" came the reply. The lady, still shrouded in the darkness of the bedroom, sat up. Eyes still closed, she tried to make sense of what was happening around her. She glanced at the clock through squinting eyes and realising the time, breathed a sigh and turned towards the edge of the bed, her head hung low. She pushed her feet into her slippers by the side of her bed and slowly stood up, steadying herself for a moment with a hand on the headboard. Shuffling, she grabbed a light, silken dressing gown which was hanging from a bedpost at the foot of the bed and she pulled it on over her long night gown.

The man, still in bed, whispered, "Milk and two sugars please my darling."

This was met in response by a pillow being thrown onto the snoozing man and the muttered comment, "Cheeky bastard!" as the lady left the room, tying her dressing gown cord around her waist. The man laughed before turning over to try to get another few minutes of sleep.

No. 10 Downing Street, London. 18th March - 08:35.

In the kitchen of No.10 Downing Street, a grey-haired man in his fifties, wearing a long, brown, corduroy dressing gown sat eating toast at a table, accompanied by a cup of steaming black coffee and a glass of orange juice whilst reading one of that morning's broadsheet newspapers, his half-rim glasses balanced on the tip of his nose. The kitchen was a mix of modern and traditional. There was a large, old-style, eight hob range oven, two Belfast sinks sunk into the worktop next to each other, and a new but old-style Victorian tap hanging over the pair. The cupboards were pine-coloured, but the doors were in a shaker style with modern handles. The walls were white, with multicoloured, bright tiles around the oven and sinks, and the room was lit by downlight spots sunk into the ceiling.

The man had a kindly face with a square jawline which bore the scars and wrinkles of age. He had very short stubble across his face which had hints of white hairs coming through. The woman, a tall slim, lady, dressed in a matching maroon skirt suit and neck-length, bobbed, greying hair entered the kitchen and, in passing, took a bite out of one of the man's slices of toast from his plate. "Oi," stated the man in a soft form of disapproval. The pair smiled at one another.

"Are you ready?" asked the man, looking back to his newspaper.

"No. But then, will I ever be?" came the reply. "It's a crime John," she stated. "What he did. He should be held to account for doing it, even if it was over forty years ago."

The man, still looking down at the paper, shook his head.

"I know... I know. I just don't see the logic in it," he replied. "What good could come of it now?"

The Prime Minister was still chewing on her stolen bit of toast, whilst pulling a soft, black, woollen coat over her suit, and fastening the large, black buttons. This was followed by a thick, maroon scarf.

"He must be punished as an example," she said. "We can't have rogue veterans claiming things that could harm this country's reputation. I know it must have been hell over there, but still."

John, raising his head from the newspaper, turned to look at his wife again and pulled his glasses off his face. "I just hope it's the right decision. For you. For us, *and* for the country."

The Prime Minister smiled coyly. "Me too," she said, before leaning over John and kissing his forehead gently. "I love you. I'll see you tonight," she whispered to him.

Just then, a man dressed in a sharp, black suit, black tie and a white shirt walked into the kitchen doorway and knocked gently at the open kitchen door. "Excuse me, Prime Minister.

14

Your car is outside," he said.

"Thank you," she replied, before turning and walking out of the kitchen toward the front door.

"Roast chicken tonight!" John stated loudly, just before the front door slammed shut. "Ooh lovely," he said to himself sarcastically, now sitting on his own. "Sounds delicious. Yes please!" he continued, holding a conversation with himself.

The Prime Ministers car. 18th March - 08:50.

In the back of a large, black Jaguar car with darkened windows, the Prime Minister, Patricia Kaine, rifled through numerous documents on her lap, putting all of them in order and reciting parts of her speech which required clear and concise pronunciation. In front of the car, and behind it, were two other black cars with tinted windows and carrying Specialist Protection (S.O.1) security personnel on board, and a number of motorcycle police giving the cars an escort to Parliament; blue lights flashing but no sirens. In the front of the car was a member of the Prime Minister's security team from S.O.1. A young, fresh-faced man in his mid-twenties, cleanly shaven and perfectly combed hair with a small, clear, curled wire protruding from the back of his perfectly-ironed, white shirt collar and ending in his ear. Also there was the Prime Minister's driver, Frank Arthur. Frank had been the Prime Minister's driver for a number of years. A part of the furniture, if you will. He was an older man in his sixties with well-groomed, parted hair, greying, and he wore a smart two-piece suit and a paisley tie. He looked at his passenger through his rear-view mirror.

"Everything all right ma'am?" asked Frank. "You look,

well, dare I say a little preoccupied?"

The Prime Minister, dropping her concentration for a moment, looked back at Frank in his mirror, then looked down at her documents and smiled. "Yes, I'm fine. Thank you, Frank."

Frank averted his eyes back to the road. "Right you are ma'am." Patricia Kaine, despite having all of her speech notes and all of her evidence in her files, still felt uneasy about her appearance and speech today. Something just didn't sit right with her. The case she was about to discuss in Parliament was a very sensitive topic.

In recent years, U.K. life had become very much a blame culture. Suing each other for the smallest things was becoming a standard practice. The news ran stagnant with finger-pointing and witch hunts for every little thing. And it wasn't because the people demanded it. It was because the politicians felt that it should be done for the good of the nation.

But this case was a whole new level on the bar. The case related to a British paratrooper, Martin Jones who, alongside a number of other paras, reportedly opened fire on Northern Irish protesters in the Bogside area of Derry, Northern Ireland on the 30th January 1972, resulting in the deaths of fourteen civilians. History books are clouded by what happened that day. He said – she said. Rumors had been rife for years that in 2007, Prime Minister Tony Blair agreed to stop hunting on-the-run members of the I.R.A and Patricia Kaine knew all too well that this had been one of the biggest cover-ups in British history.

And since it was only twenty-two years since the eventual ceasefire and end to hostilities in Northern Ireland, she knew she had to tread lightly with her approach to today's case in the Houses of Parliament. Many of the members of the house on all sides of the argument were ex-serving members of the military. Some had served in Northern Ireland during the troubles. She knew that today's discussion was a volatile subject that required a softly-softly approach, so as not to cause anger or chaos both within the house, or out in public. She sat, contemplating what she was about to do, in silence, as the cavalcade made its final approach to the Houses of Parliament.

CHAPTER TWO
BETRAYAL

The Houses of Parliament, London. 18th March - 09:00.

The Prime Minister's car and supporting vehicles arrived outside the Houses of Parliament. They idled up to the entrance very slowly before lazily pulling to a stop.

"Good luck ma'am. I'm sure you'll handle today's discussion with distinction – as always," said Frank, looking back at the Prime Minister over his shoulder as he turned off the ignition. She looked back at Frank and leaned forwards, placing her hand on his shoulder, and with a coy smile replied, "Thank you, Frank." Her S.O.1 security operative exited the vehicle as soon as the car had come to a stop, and had a good look around. He closed his door and fastened his suit jacket buttons and arranged his tie before opening the Prime Minister's door.

"I'll see you at lunchtime Frank." Holding on tightly to her notes and files, she tucked them all neatly under her arm as she quickly exited the vehicle and the S.O.1 operative closed the rear door behind her.

"True Blue has exited the vehicle," said the S.O.1 operative with a finger in his ear, as he and the Prime Minister walked away from the car. True Blue was S.O.1's codename for the Prime Minister.

The moment she left the vehicle, dozens of British

reporters, already waiting there, began shouting and swarming like flies around the metal barriers set up to keep a path open for arriving personnel. A constant stream of camera flashes and the sounds of cameras clicking away were all around her. She kept her head down and avoided any eye-contact with the reporters as she made her way into the Houses of Parliament. Shouts from reporters all around rang in her ears.

"Prime Minister! Prime Minister! Are you doing the right thing? Prime Minister! Are you ashamed of what you're about to do? Prime Minister! Do you have any comment or statement to make?" She ignored them all. An aide to the Prime Minister appeared at the door from inside, passed her and stood behind the Prime Minister, addressing the press. "There will be a statement made after this morning's proceedings!" he stated, holding his hands up to the press in an attempt to silence their shouts and block the Prime Minister from the view of photographers. The Prime Minister continued on her way in. She lifted her head and stared straight ahead. A small smile appeared on her face as she carried on her quick walk into the Houses of Parliament, escorted by her security operative who helped by clearing her path of straying M.P.s and press.

Once inside, she made sure she was out of sight of the reporters and took a deep breath. There, she was met by her Deputy Prime Minister, Richard Baker.

"Welcome Prime Minister. As you can see, we rolled out the red carpet for your arrival," he joked as they shook hands. Patricia's security operative stopped just behind her. He held his hands together in front of him, as he scanned the entrance-way and halls from left to right and back again.

"Yes, I can see you did. Thank you, Richard" Patricia joked, an uncomfortable smile appeared on her face.

Richard Baker was a short man. He was shorter than

Patricia by a good foot. He was aged around forty years old. He was cleanly shaven, with short, trimmed hair, all black.

He was slim and wore a very smart and fashionable grey three-piece suit, fitted, and a paisley tie against a white shirt.

Patricia's tone lowered. "How are feelings in the House this morning?" she asked, as they slowly turned and began to walk.

As they passed through the Commons Corridor and The House Lobby, Richard replied. "Tense, Prime Minister. *Very* tense. On both sides of the room." Richard was looking in all directions as he walked, speaking softly, making sure nobody was listening.

Richard Baker stopped and turning to face her, held the Prime Minister's arm gently. causing her to stop suddenly and turn to face him. He leaned in towards her and said quietly, "Look, Patricia. I know you believe you're doing the right thing here. Many don't. And as for me, well you know me. I've already followed you to hell and back… but, are you sure you want to do this? Are you sure this is the right direction? For you, I mean. For the party? There is still time to change your mind."

The Prime Minister thought for a moment, looking at Richard with a somewhat confused look on her face. "If I didn't know better Richard, I'd think you were *trying* to change my mind," she said with a small smile. She shrugged her arm slightly and Richard let go of his soft grip. She continued. "Yes, I believe now is the time. I have been given this responsibility by the people of Britain. I cannot and will not let them down."

Richard looked the Prime Minister in the eyes and with a small, knowing nod and smile, admitted defeat. He stood up straight and placed his hand on Patricia's shoulder. "Then so be it Prime Minister. Let's go and make history." They both turned and carried on walking together.

House of Commons Chamber, The Houses of Parliament. 18th March - 09:10.

The Prime Minister paused outside the chambers for a moment. "I'll see you inside," Richard said, as he passed by her and carried on in. He made his way to his seat through a handful of M.P.s who were stood idly chatting in the chamber. The big, black, wooden doors to the chamber were wide open and she could see almost everybody inside. Before entering, she took a deep breath. She knew this debate would be televised live to millions around the country. It was a massive debate, so she would expect nothing less. What she was more worried about was making her point, yet still keeping on the good side of Parliament *and* the public. She wanted to make sure that she wasn't depicted as the ogre or 'Angel of Death', as some of the tabloids and news outlets were daubing her as. She was determined to make a solid point on this subject and the veteran para had to be made an example of, yet she still had to retain the respect of the House and the Armed Forces in general. They too, were watching very, very closely.

"Five minutes, Prime Minister," said Marcus Aldridge, the Speaker of the House of Commons as he passed Patricia in the hallway. They exchanged smiles as he passed. It was time. She held her head high, took a deep breath and took her first steps into the chamber.

As she left the relative safety of the darkened entrance-way, the lights from the chamber lit her face. M.P.s around the chamber turned to watch her enter and she was met by a mixture of M.P.s banging on benches as a sign of support, and boos which rang throughout the chamber. She didn't let that phase her though. This had happened to her on more than one occasion. Walking tall, she headed straight to her seat and kept her focus.

"Order! Order!" rang out across the Chamber from the Speaker as he reached his seat. Silence slowly fell across the chamber after a few moments, just at the stroke of 09:30. All members had taken their seats, but it was so packed in the chamber that a good few had to stand. And, as the last of the whispers died down, the Speaker of the House began.

"Order! Order! This morning, Monday 18th March 2019, we are discussing the case and trial for murder, of Paratrooper Martin Jones which occurred on the 30th January 1972. I hand the floor to the Right Honorable Prime Minister, Patricia Kaine."

The Prime Minister stood and approached the table, whilst being hailed and heckled simultaneously from all directions. She placed her speech notes on the table and opened a file containing her speech. She looked around. The sound of the House Members was deafening. She noticed the cameras which hung from the ceiling above were all pointing directly at her. She knew they were on, all cameras lit with a small red L.E.D. and that her picture was being beamed live across the country. She looked at the faces of the M.P.s on the opposite benches. Some waiting in anticipation. Some slowly shaking their heads in disagreement. Some just looking down at the floor, waiting for the talking to begin. The noise around her died down, before there was silence and she looked down at her speech and opened her mouth to speak her first words.

Suddenly, across the chamber, various Members of Parliament silently stood. The Prime Minister paused and lifted her head, having noticed movement from the corner of her eye. They all stood in unison and before the speech could go any further, those standing M.P.s began to make their way through the crowds of other M.P.s and out through the large, black, main doors of the chamber. There was confusion in the chamber. Whispers rose. The Prime Minister didn't quite know what to do. She stood and watched as thirty-five members across all parties, including the Deputy Prime Minister himself, silently walked out of the chamber. Richard Baker threw a single glance back at the Prime Minister as he walked. He seemed embarrassed. Patricia Kaine and the majority of the remaining Members of the House were shocked. Whispers grew around the chamber as they all left and the doors closed behind them.

"Order! Order!" shouted the Speaker, almost screaming, trying to calm the chatter. The Prime Minister, eyes wide, obviously shocked, still unsure as to what had just happened, felt betrayed by Richard Baker's actions. She felt like he'd just lied to her face, then stabbed her in the back. But she didn't want to look like a fool, a weak fool at that, in front of the remaining M.P.s and the television cameras, so stood tall and decided to carry on.

"Order Ladies and Gentlemen … *ORDER!*" came the shouts from the Speaker once more. It took a good five minutes for the talking and chatter to eventually die down. The Prime Minister having regained her composure, began to talk.

House of Commons Chamber, The Houses of Parliament. 18th March– 09:20.

"Mr. Speaker, Ladies, Gentlemen and Right Honorable Members of the House. Today is a day of reckoning. A day of truth. A day of…"

And with that, every live TV feed fell silent. Sky News, B.B.C., Al Jazeera, C.N.N., I.T.V., Fox. Every news feed streaming the debate live stopped, and the screens went blank. People watching around the country and the world were puzzled. News channels returned to their studio-based anchors.

"Well, we seem to have lost the feed. We'll try and get it back as soon as possible," they all stated, fumbling pieces of paper on the desks before them.

What they didn't know was that they wouldn't get it back.

CHAPTER THREE
DELIVERANCE

In the centre of London, a massive explosion erupted through the roof of the Houses of Parliament, like a dormant volcano billowing back to life. The force of the blast was so powerful that Queen Elizabeth Tower, holding Big Ben, collapsed, ejecting the bell out through the face of the clock. The eruption tore upwards and outwards in all directions. A split-second later, the massive shock wave produced by the explosion hit nearby buildings, blowing out windows and knocking people clean off their feet. Thousands of pigeons and birds flew in panic from every high-rise building for miles in every direction as the shockwave increased in size. Car alarms began in unison as their windscreens and windows were blown away. Cars passing Parliament were flipped onto their sides and roofs like toy cars with the force of the explosion. People within a few hundred metres of the Houses of Parliament cowered as they were showered in debris, shrapnel and glass. Stone and dust rained down across at least a one-kilometer radius around the explosion. The blast knocked tourists off their feet in every one of the pods hanging from the London Eye, as they all rocked back and forth with the force. The entire structure wobbled and swayed from one side to the other in the blast wave. Luckily, all but one of the cables holding it upright held tight. Only one cable snapped, which whipped across the giant wheel, narrowly missing a pod. Thick dust filled the air and rolled across the River Thames and down adjoining streets like a slow-moving steam roller, covering everything in dust and blocking out the sun turning day into night. A news helicopter passing nearby was rocked by the shock wave of the explosion. Numerous red alarm lights illuminated on the control panel in front of the pilot, with a series of warning alarms sounding. "Warning. Warning. Stall. Stall." It repeated. The pilot, fighting to keep the helicopter in the air, managed to wrestle control. Upon looking down, it was like a scene from a war movie. The Houses of Parliament were completely destroyed and flames lapped every section of the remaining structure. A passenger in the helicopter screamed into the radio, calling for help to attend as soon as possible, and describing the scene below him to whoever would listen whilst a cameraman in the back of the helicopter picked himself up from the floor and shakily started to take footage.

On the ground, people were beginning to pick themselves up. They were shell-shocked. Confused. Dazed. Everyone's hearing was impaired with constant ringing following the explosion. Some wandered aimlessly, coughing, some sat crying quietly, rocking back and forth. Some ran around screaming looking for loved ones. One man emerged from the dust, crying and carrying his unconscious wife in his arms, asking for help as blood and dust covered them both. Everybody was covered from head to foot in thick dust. Those who could help, did. People rallied around, helping collect the injured or dying from the streets and into shelter utilising nearby doorways, alleyways and shops, covering their faces with coats, shirts, scarves or whatever they could find to help keep the dust out of their eyes and lungs.

Although hindered by dust clouds, emergency services

reacted following hundreds of calls and reached the scene quickly. Dozens of ambulances, police cars and fire engines began appearing through the dust clouds with police and paramedics treating the injured outside of the Houses of Parliament. An Air Ambulance managed to land nearby on Parliament Square Garden, blowing up plumes of dust from the grass. Firefighters tried to tackle the blaze within the House itself which was roaring, attempting to soak a path inside to check and search for survivors, but it was impossible. The Houses of Parliament were so old that the fire had already taken too much of a hold to put out anytime soon. The old, wooden beams burned like kindling, sparking and ejecting floating embers as it crackled. Firefighters tried to get into the ruins as colleagues focused their water cannons at certain locations. However, every attempt failed as rubble fell and blocked their paths, and whichever location they attempted to get through, the problems remained the same. They just couldn't get in. All they could do was wait for the fire to burn itself out and the rubble to stop falling.

Anybody on the inside was on their own for now.

CHAPTER FOUR
NEEDLE IN A HAYSTACK

Central London. 19th March - 12:34.

The remains of the Houses of Parliament were still billowing white and grey smoke, even after more than twenty-four hours, but the flames were gone. Burning embers smouldered deep inside the remains and the smoke rose into the London sky of another sunny day. However, today was much, much different. The Houses of Parliament lay in ruins.

The Metropolitan Police Force had cordoned off the area to a safe distance of a few hundred metres. Armed Police and the Army were deployed to patrol Central London and secure the remains of Parliament, keeping civil order and maintaining the peace. Forensic experts scoured the remains of the Houses of Parliament and surrounding areas that were deemed safe enough to investigate, looking for the tiniest clues, whilst the Fire Brigade remained on site, trying to put out the last of the burning embers, adorned in protective clothing and breathing apparatus. News crews from around the world surrounded the remains from all angles.

The number of dead or missing was yet to be fully established, although an estimate of between three hundred and eighty-four and four hundred was being reported by various news agencies. Nothing official had as yet, been announced.

Sections of the building remained standing. The odd old, solid wall here and there, but there wasn't enough to think of rebuilding. Over the last twenty-four hours, life in Britain had taken a very dark turn, and the feeling within the country was distinctly morose.

Parliament, having been completely destroyed and the Prime Minister missing, presumed dead, along with the majority of the British Government, meant that the leadership of the country fell automatically back with Her Royal Highness Queen Elizabeth II. However, Buckingham Palace remained silent for now.

Messages of support were flooding to the U.K. from the leaders of the free world. But with the lack of any news coming back from inside the Metropolitan Police or from Her Majesty, the public were becoming restless. However, actions were in motion behind the scenes.

Central London. 19th March – 12:58.

A cavalcade of blacked-out mini buses and vehicles arrived at the gates of Buckingham Palace which was flying all of its rooftop flags at half-mast. Each vehicle, queueing patiently one by one, was stringently inspected by the Army for explosive devices, each occupant thoroughly searched. Each bag, mobile phone and bottle of water examined closely whilst those wanting to enter were held at raised gunpoint until cleared to pass. The vehicles were intricately examined for any kinds of device attached underneath by rolling large, circular mirrors along the underneath of the vehicles whilst armed troops searched the interiors thoroughly, and sniffer dogs circled the vehicles from outside, guided by their handlers. The

Palace were taking no chances and had tripled the number of Army personnel on site.

Once cleared, the vehicles moved slowly in unison through the grounds of Buckingham Palace and all pulled up to the rear of the Palace. The doors to the vehicles opened and all the occupants emerged once more and were quickly ushered into the Palace by security services. At the head of the group was Richard Baker, the Deputy Prime Minister followed closely by the other thirty-four Members of Parliament that had walked out of the House minutes before the explosion. Inside the Palace, the group were quickly guided through Buckingham Palace by various armed members of S.O.1 and the military until at last, a large pair of double doors were opened and inside sat Queen Elizabeth II surrounded by a number of armed security personnel, and a couple of what appeared to be high-ranking military officials.

The Queen, not in her usual finery, was dressed in a long, black skirt suit with black hat. She sat writing at an antique, leather-topped desk on a gold, gilded, high-backed chair, whilst the military officials spoke softly to her nearby. The room was lit by amazingly tall windows that allowed ample natural sunlight to flood the room. The sunlight reflected brightly on most surfaces, and highlighted the highly polished wooden floors and gold, gilded, doorways and furniture. The windows were spotlessly clean and not a single smudge was visible. The visitors squinted their eyes to adjust to the amounts of light in the room as they entered one at a time.

"Your expected visitors, Your Majesty," said her aide, who looked up as the M.P.s walked through the doors. The whispering and talking in the room suddenly fell silent, as everyone in the room paused and turned to watch all the visitors walk in. The Queen paused for a second, and then replaced the lid of her writing pen and screwed it closed. She slowly placed it down on top of the document she was writing and turned in her chair to face the incoming visitors, lowering her glasses to the end of her nose to look over the top.

Upon realising who he stood before, Richard Baker slowed. His eyes widened and his mouth suddenly felt very dry. He was dressed all in black, apart from a white shirt. He knew who he was coming to meet at the Palace, but now he was actually stood before the Queen, he faltered a little and his heart rate increased as he felt a small bead of sweat begin to form on his brow. He stopped a good few feet in front of the Queen when instructed by one of her armed escorts, one hand raised and the other resting on the hilt of his holstered pistol. "Stop right there," he commanded. Richard Baker, his eyes flitting between the Queen and her security detail stopped and bowed. "Your Majesty," he declared.

The Queen stood, stepped forward a pace and slipped her glasses off her face, allowing them to hang on a chain around her neck.

"Mr. Baker. I thank you so very much for coming at such short notice." Richard Baker slowly raising himself from his bow, replied.

"Of course, Your Majesty." The Queen continued to talk.

"As I'm sure you are aware, our country and democracy are in grave danger. With the Prime Minister's location and condition currently unknown, and the majority of the Cabinet with her presumed lost in the Parliament explosion, we find ourselves at an impasse. Mr. Baker, we need to maintain a working government and civil control. That is why you are here. Will you, at least temporarily take the mantle of Prime

Minister of Great Britain, and form a new Government?"

Richard Baker had a feeling that this was the question she was going to ask. It didn't take him long to respond.

"I am truly honoured, Your Majesty." He paused, then stuttered. "I… fully understand the undertaking of which you are asking of me, Your Majesty. I will begrudgingly take on the roll until a more suitable replacement can be found and appointed, and I will do my very best to lead the country until such time that my services are no longer required." He took a step backwards and bowed again.

"Thank you, Mr. Baker," said the Queen. "I have no doubt you will perform a necessary, valuable and thorough job."

However, whilst Richard Baker and the other M.P.s were at Buckingham Palace, others were looking at them with suspicious eyes. He, *and* the other Members of Parliament that walked out just before the explosion.

Less than a mile from Buckingham Palace, Richard Baker's photo was attached to a pin-board in an office in Scotland Yard. The board was huge and was made up of a number of smaller pin boards all next to each other. On the boards were the photos of numerous people, Richard Baker included. The other pictures included those of the other thirty-four Members of Parliament, which were all under suspicion as they had all evaded death the day before by walking out of Parliament just before the explosion.

Work in Scotland Yard was well under way to clean up the mess left by the explosion the day before. It was close enough to blow out the majority of the windows facing the Houses of Parliament. Numerous offices were cordoned off as unsafe and were being attended by cleaners and tradesman as they went office to office, cleaning up glass from the floors, securing ceiling and walls and temporarily boarding up unsecured windows. In another office, C.C.T.V. from various locations around Parliament was being scrutinised. People going in. People coming out. People passing. People talking. Every face, no matter how long or short they were in shot – *ALL* were being investigated and run through face recognition software. Cars and registrations. Luggage, rucksacks, briefcases, bins, plastic bags, plastic bottles, mobile phones, anyone with headphones… nothing was being left to chance.

CHAPTER FIVE
DEAD ENDS

Central London. 20th March - 09:22.

As the next day broke, so did news of a State Funeral for Prime Minister Patricia Kaine. Her body, which had been recovered late the previous evening under a flood-lit search, was too damaged to lay in state in an open casket. It had been decided that she would lay in state at St. Paul's Cathedral for seven days, where visitors and mourners could come and pay their respects and sign books of condolence. This had been arranged for twelve o'clock today. Official reports indicated that, although clear that the Prime Minister had died as a result of the explosion and subsequent fire, there was no way of finding an official cause of death due to the state of the body itself. However, following the early morning breaking news, hundreds of mourners already lined the streets leading to St. Paul's Cathedral waiting to pass by the casket and pay their respects. News agencies also reported the final number of dead. Three hundred and ninety-eight people died including the Prime Minister. Three hundred and sixty-five of those had been inside the Houses of Parliament – mostly M.P.s, but included aides and a chef. The remaining thirty-three people were outside of Parliament including police officers, security guards, civilians, tourists and members of the press. All were in the wrong place, at the wrong time.

The investigation into the explosion and deaths of three hundred and ninety-eight people had been handed to Detective Chief Inspector Gillian Harper. D.C.I. Harper had been in the Metropolitan Police for a number of years and she had investigated a mixture of major crimes including murder, money laundering, armed robbery and rape. However, this was her first possible 'terrorist'-related investigation. Gillian Harper was forty-five years old, and tall. She stood about six foot two inches and was of athletic build. She had long, straight, brunette hair which flowed down between her shoulders in a pony tail. Her attire was very plain but functional. Today, it was a beige trouser suit with flat, black shoes. She was a beautiful woman, but she had a steely face that people thought would look strange with a smile, as she donned one so little. She wore no make-up and no jewellery. She didn't really need to as her skin was smooth and unblemished. Her voice was strong and her attitude matched perfectly. She said things as she saw them and many officers didn't appreciate her 'straight talking'. But her senior officers loved her. She got jobs done, and that's why she was put in charge of this investigation. This was undoubtedly the most important British investigation in generations and the Police and Security Services needed a result, and fast. If anyone was going to go out and get one, it would be her.

Gillian Harper had already begun her investigation. She'd already ordered the forensic investigation in the Houses of Parliament and made sure C.C.T.V. was scrutinised intently. Her team had constructed the pin boards and filled them with possible suspects, who at the moment consisted of the thirty-five surviving members of Parliament. On the opposite wall were more pin boards. These boards were filled with individuals who had lost their lives. These boards had many more pictures on. By each suspect's photograph, was a small piece of paper with information about each one of them. The same applied for the victims' boards. Name, age, date of birth, place of birth, address. Some were populated going on identification found in the rubble. Others were blank because they simply didn't know who they were yet. There were pieces of string, linking between suspect's photos, each with a tag with more information, trying to find connections that may be of some help. Gillian Harper had now issued orders to her team to dig deep into each of their histories, looking for anything that could highlight motives for this atrocity.

D.C.I. Harpers team was big. She had two Detective Sergeants working for her. She also had a small team of around fifteen people, working on details and background checks on her behalf.

She had access to staff within both the Forensics department and those working on the C.C.T.V.

In her pocket, D.C.I. Harper kept a notebook. Not a particularly special notebook, but a plain, old, small pocket notebook. One which you could pick up in any supermarket or corner shop. This one was plain yellow in colour with no pictures or markings of any kind. In this notebook she had her own list of suspects. She referred to it regularly. But on this list, she kept notes that maybe didn't make the pin-boards. Small things that seemed trivial, even unnecessary, but she was thorough and didn't want to miss anything. She updated her notebook often, and nobody else got to see inside it or any of her notes.

Her list of suspects so far, comprised the following Members of Parliament:

Richard Baker – Conservative and Deputy Prime Minister. Born London. Aged forty

Helen Weston – Conservative. Born Warrington. Aged forty-six.

Roberta Heathcotte – Conservative. Born Lychfield. Aged thirty-nine.

David Marfield – Conservative. Born Canterbury. Aged forty-five.

Anna Fielding – Conservative. Born Darlington. Aged fifty-six.

Hakim Sing – Conservative. Born India. Aged forty-four.

Alison Verity – Conservative. Born Hull. Aged forty-two.

Andrew Fallows – Conservative. Born London. Aged Fifty-seven.

Diane McDonald – Conservative. Born Manchester. Aged thirty-nine.

Phillip Marks – Labour. Born Cardiff. Aged fifty-two.

Gordon Fitzpatrick – Labour. Born Nottingham. Aged forty-three.

Sarah Walker – Labour. Born Stockton. Aged forty-six.

Steven Cartington – Labour. Born London. Aged fifty-six.

Jenny Willow – Labour. Born Chesterfield. Aged thirty-four.

Beverley Carmichael – Labour. Born Macclesfield. Aged fifty-four.

Martin Holdsworth – Labour. Born Liverpool. Aged forty-six.

Harvey Scott-Phillips – Labour. Born Watford. Aged thirty-eight.

Richard Marksman – Labour. Born Warrington. Aged fifty-nine.

Stuart Dorchester – Labour. Born Aldershot. Aged forty-three.

Michael Leighton – Labour. Born Glasgow. Aged forty-two.

Edward Davidson – Liberal Democrat. Born Liverpool. Aged fifty-four.

Rachael Powell – Liberal Democrat. Born Truro. Aged thirty-eight.

David Brown – Liberal Democrat. Born Swansea. Aged sixty-three.

Paul Burnett – Liberal Democrat. Born Newcastle Upon Tyne. Aged forty-five.

Claire White – Liberal Democrat. Born Carlisle. Aged forty-four.

Andrew Simpson – Liberal Democrat. Born Leeds. Aged thirty-none.

Jocelyn Bailey – Liberal Democrat. Born Chester. Aged forty-eight.

Ben Martin-Walker – Liberal Democrat. Born London. Aged sixty-four.

Lewis Marshall – Green Party. Born Bridlington. Aged forty

William Newton – Green Party. Born Grimsby. Aged forty-two

Claudia Royce – Green Party. Born Milton Keynes. Aged thirty-seven.

Michael Schmidt – Green Party. Born Dover. Aged forty-three.

Chris Samuels – Green Party. Born Harrington. Aged fifty-four.

Joanne Sedgewick – Green Party. Born Windsor. Aged sixty-one.
Matilda Montrose – Independent Party. Born Huddersfield. Aged thirty-four.

This was D.C.I. Harper's initial list. She expected it to get bigger day by day, but this was the list she wanted to focus on first.

CHAPTER SIX
MAKING ENDS MEET

Scotland Yard. 20th March - 11:00.

D.C.I. Gillian Harper's team were constantly looking at C.C.T.V., photographs, Social Media and mobile phone footage from members of the public trying to find anything to help their investigation but so far, no one they could pursue as a credible suspect. A few faces had been flagged by the facial recognition software but only for minor misdemeanors such as shoplifting, common assault, speeding, drink driving. Nothing to the scale of bomb making, terrorism or murder. So far, they were coming up short. D.C.I. Harper knew she had to get some movement on this investigation.

The public were baying for answers, as were the press, not to mention her bosses.

D.C.I. Harper called two officers into her office.

"D.S. Pierce! D.S. Cope! Come in here please!" Two officers entered her office. "Close the door please Mike," She said. Detective Sergeant Mike Pierce closed the door behind him and walked towards the desk where Gillian Harper sat. Both men were thin. They wore suits which looked like they were a couple of years old with white shirts and loose ties, the shirts unbuttoned at the top. D.S. Pierce had short, blonde hair which was very short around the sides and back. He had a stony look on his face, with designer stubble all over his cheeks and face. He bore a couple of small scars on his forehead. D.S. Cope had dark brown hair. It was cut short all over and he had a poorly trimmed beard.

D.C.I. Harper's office was bland. Basic. A desk, a black, leather chair, a phone, a computer and a stack of paperwork and files. There was a window in need of a good clean but at least it was in one piece, unlike some of the others in the building. It came with a view of a busy road. The walls were magnolia in colour and bare, apart from a couple of commendation certificates and newspaper clippings behind her desk, and a small flat screen T.V. behind the door showing Sky News permanently.

"Take a seat Mike, Rich. I need you two to start questioning these M.P.s. I know there's a few and it will take you a while. But time is ticking. We need to start eliminating some of these from our enquiries. As you know, I've got the rest of the team working day and night looking through footage, C.C.T.V., Twitter, Facebook, Instagram, news agencies and my grandmother's knicker drawer! I also have a team on the ground waiting for any forensic information as it comes to light." She sat for a moment, looking thoughtfully at the two men, and sipping from a barely warm cup of coffee. "I need something. Anything. Why did they leave the building? Where were they going? Body language. Expressions. Eye contact. Sweat. Restlessness. I want history from each of them. Holidays. Marriages. Family. Friends. Drinking haunts. Shoe size and favourite ice-cream flavours! Leave nothing to chance!"

D.S. Mike Pierce replied. "No problem, boss. Leave it with us. We'll start with the Deputy Prime Minister. C'mon Rich, let's go." The two men stood up, fastened their suit

41

jackets, tucked away their ties and left the room, closing the office door behind them.

D.C.I. Harper knew she could trust these men. She'd worked with them for about eight years and they had never let her down. Both men knew in the early days that Gillian would advance well in the Met. They knew her detective skills far outweighed their own and that her judgement was always sound and they followed her orders without question.

St. Paul's Cathedral. 20th March 2019 - 11:55.

D.S.s Pierce and Cope arrived at St. Paul's Cathedral and stopped their car about fifty yards short of the entrance. It was a plain, silver Vauxhall Vectra with no distinguishing markings. It fitted in very well as a bland, old, unmarked police car.

As they got out, an armed police officer on patrol approached the pair. "Sorry gents no parking here."

The pair took out their I.D.s and proceeded to show them to the armed officer, as they closed the car doors. "We're here to have a word with the Deputy Prime Minister, once he's paid his respects of course," said D.S. Cope.

"Sorry Detective Sergeant – yes of course. He's right at the front of the queue with the other M.P.s." The armed officer pointed out the crowd outside of St. Paul's. "They'll be heading in right after the P.M.'s family when it opens, which should be in just a minute," said the armed officer, glancing at his watch.

"Thanks. We'll be out of your hair as soon as possible," said D.S. Pierce. The officer smiled and with a nod, moved off and carried on patrolling the street.

"We'll wait until he's out. Then we'll ask if he wouldn't mind having a word," said D.S. Pierce, as the pair of them leaned next to each other, cross armed on the bonnet of the car.

"It might be a bit embarrassing for him, in front of all the other M.P.s." said D.S. Cope.

"I'm sure it will, but we have to do our job. And, as he has nothing to hide. I'm sure he'll be more than willing to help," said D.S. Pierce. They got up and slowly walked towards the door that the M.P.s would use to exit St. Paul's, and waited.

The door to St. Paul's Cathedral opened. The Metropolitan Police allowed the family members in first, followed by the M.P.s, guests and VIPs shortly after, holding the general public back until St. Paul's was empty once more. Leading the family line was her husband Richard, and his two grown sons. All three in deep mourning. The sons, both around nineteen years of age, followed on behind Richard, holding each other up with tears running down their faces. They paused at the coffin and Richard held both of his sons whilst they all cried together.

After a while, once the family of Patricia Kaine had paid their respects, Richard Baker led the M.P.s into the Great Hall. They were all dressed in black and walked slowly, hands together in front of them and heads bowed. Either side of the entrance behind metal barriers, the press captured every second. There was no talking at all. Inside it was completely silent except for the soft tones of distant organ music. Stainless steel bollards with ropes had been positioned to guide all visitors through the hall and passed the casket. The hall inside seemed dim due to the dull weather and not much natural light came through the windows, but inside it remained beautiful. Dozens of candles were lit and placed around the casket and on surrounding walls and tables. Amazing paintings adorned the grand arches within St. Paul's. Draped across the casket was a large Union Jack flag and stationed either side of the coffin stood military guards in their finest attire with rifles. On the visitor's side of the rope, on either side of the display was a stand, and on each stand was a Book of Condolence. Attached by a fine silk rope to each book was a beautiful, silver pen which everyone could use to sign.

The M.P.s stopped directly in between the stands holding the books of condolence. They formed a small group of three deep and stood in silent contemplation for a number of minutes. Some held handkerchiefs up to their noses, tears running down their cheeks. Others just stood in silent contemplation, staring at the casket. Then, slowly, one by one they signed the books starting with Richard Baker. Richard signed the book nearest to him. He wrote:

'Patricia, words cannot express the sadness and pain that your passing has left on the people of this great nation. You've given everything in sacrifice to your country. Your legacy will live on forever more. Yours, Richard Baker.'

He replaced the pen lid, and gently lay the pen on the center crease of the open book and started to move slowly towards the exit on his own, whilst the other M.P.s remained to sign the books. Before he reached the exit, he turned and faced the casket one last time. He drew a deep breath. He knew inside that the task he had been given was massive and he didn't want to let the people of Britain or the Queen down. He bowed his head in respect to Patricia, and turned to leave.

St. Paul's Cathedral. 20th March - 12:30.

"Mr. Richard Baker?" asked D.S. Pierce, as Richard Baker left St. Paul's Cathedral. He looked up at the pair of police officers as he exited St. Paul's.

"Actually, it's 'Prime Minister'," he responded, his eyes moving between the pair of officers.

"Oh – excuse *me* sir. I'm D.S. Pierce, this is D.S. Cope. We're from Scotland Yard. We wanted to have a word if you could spare a few minutes?" he said, as the pair showed their I.D.'s.

Richard Baker nodded. He undid the buttons on his suit jacket and placed his hands in his pockets. "I had a feeling you'd want a word at some point. Yes – I suppose so." Mike Pierce turned slightly and still looking at Richard Baker, gestured with his hand towards the car. Richard Baker followed D.S. Pierce's hand with his eyes and having seen the car, nodded and walked between the pair of officers towards the car.

"So, Prime Minister. When did that happen? I don't recall hearing about that on the news," said D.S. Cope.

"Yesterday," Richard responded, "although it hasn't been made public just yet, and I'd like it to stay that way. At least for now." The pair of police officers, walking slightly behind Richard Baker, looked at each other and each gave a small smile.

"Of course, Prime Minister," came the reply from D.S. Cope. Mike Pierce sped up a little and reached to open the rear door of the Vauxhall Vectra for the Prime Minister. Richard Baker had a quick look around to make sure nobody was watching, and quickly sat in the back of the car. Mike closed the door, then the two officers proceeded to climb into the front of the car before slowly pulling away.

CHAPTER SEVEN
REALISATION

New Scotland Yard. 20th March - 13:45.

D.S.s Pierce and Cope sat in an interview room on the opposite side of a table to Richard Baker. The room was small. It had a table, a few old, red, plastic, molded chairs and plain, grey walls. There was another smaller table with a recording device on it. The room didn't have a window and was lit with an old strip-light which flickered intermittently, and gave off an annoying, low-level buzzing noise. The interview had been going on for a while.

"So, Prime Minister. Can you tell me again why you and thirty-four other Members of Parliament walked out of the Houses of Parliament just moments before the explosion?" asked Rich.

"Yes, as I said earlier. We'd all decided beforehand that if Patricia was to go ahead with her statement that morning, the thirty-five of us would walk out in protest. What she was doing was *not* by any means a popular decision amongst the Members of the House. We simply didn't agree that what she was doing was the right course of action. Those of us that stood and left, were making our own point to her," Richard Baker replied.

"And don't you think, Prime Minister, that it may look a little, well, *suspicious* that you all walked out just before the building was destroyed?" asked Mike.

"Yes, I can see why you'd say that. But let me reassure you both that it was sheer good-luck on our part that we did. I have e-mails on my phone going back *weeks* which show conversations between many of the thirty-five involved that this was always going to be the plan. And it's not as if we all got off 'Scott Free' as it were. We might have left the building, but we were all showered in debris, we're all suffering ear and hearing problems. We were all blown off our feet and thrown across the street! I believe one of our party even broke an arm. I'm surprised none of us were killed but we could have been!" Richard Baker said.

Mike sat forwards and looked at his watch, then at Rich.

"Would you like a drink Prime Minister? Coffee, tea, water?" Richard Baker nodded.

"Coffee please. White, two sugars thanks."

The officers stood up. "Interview paused for a break," said Rich Cope, before pausing the recorder and turning to face the door.

"We'll be right back," Rich said as they left the room.

Mike Pierce closed the door once Rich had left the room. They walked a few steps down the corridor and stopped to face one another. "He seems clean," said Mike quietly, looking around. "Fool proof alibi." Rich nodded.

"Yep. He's calm. His body language seems to indicate he's telling the truth. All the answers marry up. First impressions are he's not involved." Mike nodded. "You get his coffee. I'll have a quick word with D.C.I. Harper. Let her know how we're getting on," said Mike, and they both went their separate ways.

There was a knock at the door. "Come in," came the reply. Mike Pierce entered and closed the door behind him.

"Ah – Mike. Take a seat," said Gillian. Mike pulled back a chair in front of Gillian's desk and took a seat.

"I wanted to give you an update on Richard Baker. He's in interrogation now," said Mike. "Did you know he's now 'Prime Minister'?" Mike asked, as he undid his jacket button and took a seat.

Gillian stopped typing on her keyboard and looked at Mike. "Really? No – I didn't know that."

"There's more," said Mike. "I think he's clean." Gillian's eyebrows lifted. "It turns out that he, and the other thirty-four Members of Parliament had decided to walk out in protest of Patricia Kaine's decision to pursue a charge of murder against that old Paratrooper veteran, and his part in the events of Bloody Sunday back in 1972. It's been all over the news in recent weeks," said Mike. "Apparently, they'd all agreed weeks ago that if she was going to pursue it, they would all walk out in protest."

Gillian, listening intently to Mike, brought up a question. "Is there evidence to prove this?" she asked.

"Yes, there's evidence to suggest this was planned a while ago. He's shown us the emails amongst various M.P.s planning this, via his mobile phone. Obviously, it was all kept 'hush hush' but whoever set off that bomb didn't know they were going to miss thirty-five Members of Parliament. I think it was pure luck that they walked out before it went off."

Gillian sat back in her chair. "That's one hell of a stroke

of luck, isn't it?" she asked.

"We'll have to interview the others, but I feel it may be the same story. We'll keep looking and update you as we go," said Mike.

Gillian, in deep thought, her hands up to her face, nodded slightly. "Thanks Mike. Wrap it up as soon as possible and get him out of here. You'll move onto the next M.P. as soon as you can."

Suddenly, there was a loud knock on the door. "Come in!" shouted Gillian. In walked a female officer in full uniform. She seemed flustered, breathing heavily and her cheeks were red as if she'd been running. She carried a file which she immediately offered over the desk to Gillian, her eyes wide, scanning between Gillian and Mike.

"D.C.I. Harper. I have the first findings from Forensics. You may want to look at them – *now,*" she suggested.

D.C.I. Harper took the file and looked at Mike with a confused look. She placed the file down in front of her and opened it. She pulled the first few pieces of paper from the file, sat back in her chair and began to look through the documents. Her face began to express a mix of emotions. Anger being one.

"Thank you," she said to the female officer, and beckoned her to leave. She did just that, closing the door behind her.

"Mike. Get Richard Baker out of the station, now. Get Rich and meet me in the briefing room in fifteen minutes. I'll assemble the team." She stood quickly, sending her leather chair rolling backwards into the wall, and having grabbed the file, took large strides towards the door before Mike was even up out of his seat. She swung open the door and marched off down the hall carrying the file with her, telling her team to meet in the briefing room in fifteen minutes as she walked.

Mike, looking confused, left the office and headed back towards the interview rooms.

Back at the interview rooms, Mike met Rich outside of the room containing Richard Baker. "I've already given him his coffee," said Rich.

"D.C.I. Harper has something back from forensics. I don't know what but it's got her spooked. She wants us to finish up here *now*, and get over to the briefing room." Rich nodded. They turned and both walked into the interview room together.

"Well, thank you for your patience Prime Minister. We won't be needing to take up any more of your time. I think you've helped us with everything we need for now, but we may need to speak to you in the not too distant future. Will you be okay getting home?"

Richard Baker, picking up his cup of coffee, nodded.

"Yes, I'll be fine, thank you. Along with the title, I get the perks of the job, including a driver," he said, drinking the coffee down in one go. "I'll give him a ring and get him over here to collect me." He stood, leaving his empty cup on the table and fastened the button on his suit jacket. "Thank you, Detective Sergeants. I hope you manage to draw a close to this case swiftly. The country needs some answers. I hope you find them quickly." He left the room, and escorted by a uniformed officer, made his way to the exit.

Mike and Rich stood and watched as he left. "Come on, let's get over to the briefing room," said Rich.

Both Mike and Rich arrived at the briefing room only a few minutes later. Other team members were still arriving and taking their seats. The room was already filled with whispers and chatter. D.C.I. Harper stood at the front of the room, leaning up against a desk with her arms crossed, the file firmly in her hand. Mike could tell she was rattled.

The room was wide, with room for a dozen seats in a row. There were large windows letting in the light, and the room resembled D.C.I. Harper's office, just bigger. It was bland, with square ceiling tiles and strip lights once again. Non-descript coloured carpet tiles on the floor, and a projector screen on the wall.

"Come on in. Grab a cup of coffee and sit down please" Gillian said loudly as the team entered the room. Mike and Rich walked out again to a table in the next room where a hot pot of coffee had just finished brewing.

"Coffee Mike?" asked Rich.

"Of course, Rich. White, two sugars please." Rich poured two cups of coffee and they made their way back to the briefing room, and into some seats at the back of the room facing the front. The remaining members of the team soon entered and took their seats, the last one closing the briefing room door behind them. There were whispers abound in the room but they soon stopped.

"Okay! Quieten down people! We have a major development in this case! Please *SHUT UP* and listen." The room fell silent. All eyes and ears were now on D.C.I. Harper.

She began to speak.

"As of about fifteen minutes ago, this case took a much more sinister turn, ladies and gentlemen. Forensic tests from the Houses of Parliament which I have only just received, show that there seems to have been at least six explosive devices throughout the main chambers, possibly more. All detonated at *exactly* the same moment. They were *linked*, somehow. We're waiting on more test results to confirm this but…" she paused, "it looks like a professional hit. Traces of military grade explosives and detonators."

Whispers began to circulate the room. "Make no mistake ladies and gentleman. This was no amateur. Whoever did this, did so by firstly getting into Parliament and planting explosives. Lots of explosives." Gillian's hands were becoming more animated, waving around and hands grasping at the air. "Secondly, they linked them all – fuse cable, wireless, however. Thirdly, they did it *all* covertly. They got in unseen! That means passed security, passed C.C.T.V. and passed police, passed M.P.s and planted the explosives in multiple locations. Team – we need that C.C.T.V. from the Houses of Parliament. We need every second of that information checked, then rechecked for *at least* two weeks leading up to the explosion. Even further if possible." The whispers continued. D.C.I. Harper raised her voice to make sure she was heard over the chatter. "I will also be liaising with my colleagues in Special Branch, the Bomb Squad and the Security Services S.O.1." The whispers died down. "Ladies and gentleman – it is possible that this was a strike at Britain herself and her civil liberties and freedoms that she provides by another not-so-accepting country or group. At this moment in time, we have to consider this a possible act of terrorism, possibly even war. Russia. China. North Korea. Iran. The I.R.A. I.S.I.S. I cannot stress this enough people. We *need* that information." Gillian's tone lowered somewhat. "As it stands, our country is without a leader. Somebody out there decided to cut the head off the snake, which means our country is, right now, at its most vulnerable. The M.O.D. have this afternoon increased our country's security level to 'Critical' ladies and gentleman. That means another attack is now highly likely because we have no leadership. We need to find out who did this, if for no other reason than to try to stop a possible future attack." D.C.I. Harper looked around the room. It was clear that the message was sinking in. Faces all around the room were stony. She could see the emotions building up inside her team. This was exactly the response she wanted. Her voice fell back to a normal talking level. She crossed her arms, lowered her head and leant back against the desk. "We're really up against the clock now people and I know I can rely on each of you to get me some results, because I know I'm working with the best team in the Met. If this is a pre-cursor for another attack, or God forbid, war, then it's on *US* to find out who did this and give those left in government and the military the evidence *THEY* need to decide what actions to take next. You know what to do. Dismissed."

As the room cleared, D.S.s Pierce and Cope stood from their chairs and approached D.C.I. Harper at the front of the room.

"Jesus Christ, Boss," exclaimed Mike.

Gillian, still sitting on a desk at the front of the room, waited for the rest of her team to leave. She then expanded on her knowledge to her D.S.s.

"So, it looks like a vast amount of C-4 plastic explosive and Tetryl detonators. Used by the military apparently, including Britain's military as well as other countries. This wasn't some small operation. This had to have been arranged within our own borders. There's *no way* that much explosive was brought into the country from abroad. Not without raising a number of red flags. Border security is just too damn tight. It must have already been here, or been brought in in tiny amounts one trip at a time. But we need to find out from the Army if they have 'misplaced' any large amounts of plastic explosive in the last few weeks. Imagine how damaging this would be to find out that our own Prime Minister was murdered using British military supplies." Mike and Rich nodded. "I need you two to carry on interviewing each and every one of those M.P.s. One of them might just know what's going on here. You need to find them," said Gillian, clearly becoming upset. Both D.S.s nodded before leaving the room.

CHAPTER EIGHT
AN UNEXPECTED OUTCOME

New Scotland Yard.21st March - 09:15.

After a long night of going over evidence, statements, forensics and samples at her desk, D.C.I. Harper went home around midnight and that night she hadn't slept well, and had returned to the office by eight a.m. with a take-out breakfast and coffee. She sat at her desk, slowly chewing and thinking. She'd just finished a mouthful and was going in for another when the phone rang on her desk. Putting the food down and wiping her fingers with a napkin, she answered it.

"D.C.I. Harper." She listened. "I'll be right down." She slammed the phone down, leaving her half-eaten breakfast on her desk, returning only to pick up a napkin to wipe her hands further and collect her coffee before exiting the room.

Two floors down, she entered an office with a number of police officers at computers. She made her way through a maze of desks before approaching just one. A short, middle-aged man, balding with glasses and a moustache which was black but had shades of grey coming through.

"Hi William. What do you have for me?" she asked.

"Oh, hello Gillian," said the man, spinning around in his chair. "Something you're going to want to see. Take a seat." He indicated to an empty chair nearby. William Hacket had been dealing with C.C.T.V. for the Met for many years, and had helped D.C.I. Harper out numerous times before.

He turned his chair to face Gillian and leant in slightly to talk more quietly. "Okay. I've managed to retrieve some of the C.C.T.V. from Parliament. The bad news is that the majority of the equipment and hard drive have been damaged beyond repair due to the explosion and subsequent fire. The good news is that we have managed to recover something, well, significant. There is no audio I'm afraid." He turned his chair back to the computer and clicked a file. Gillian moved her chair closer to get a better view. A video window appeared – all black. But when William clicked the 'play' button, images began forming on the screen. Pixilated at first, it began to form a clearer picture. It showed the House of Parliament Chamber from a ceiling camera, pointed down the length of the chamber on a slight angle. The time in the bottom corner showed '18th March 2019 – 09:29'. Looking at the date and time of the video, she looked at William with wide eyes, slightly shocked.

"You've managed to retrieve the actual bomb going off?" she asked.

"Yes, but again there's no audio." As the video played out, William gave a running commentary of what appears to be happening.

It showed the Prime Minister standing up and moving towards the desk. She looked around at her fellow house Members. She then looked down. Before she spoke, a number of Members stood and walked out. This seemed to be one of the moments at least, that Gillian was hoping to see. "We have a number of statements so far that say this happened," said Gillian. William pressed pause on the video playback.

"Yes," said William, "but look at this door, just about... now!" William fast-forwarded the playback a few minutes before pressing play again and pointed to the main door of the chamber. It had only been closed a short number of minutes after the thirty-five M.P.s had walked out. But, just as the Prime Minister looked like she began to read from her speech, a man quickly entered the room. The large, black doors opened only slightly and a man seemed to squeeze through the small gap. He walked into the chamber a little way, seemed to say a few words, and then there was a flash of bright light and then the screen went off.

"Woah. That's horrendous. But I don't understand. What was I supposed to see?" asked Gillian.

"Let me play it back slowly for you," said William. He rewound the footage slightly and pressed slow play. The frames moved through, cycling slowly. William paused the clip. Pointing at the man in black, William began to explain his thoughts.

"Firstly, he is dressed in a long, black coat, which appears to have a medal on the left breast. Secondly, he also seems to be wearing a beret. And thirdly…" William pressed slow play again. "The explosion appears to emanate from *him!*" William pressed pause again. This time, just at a point where a bright flash is seen to be coming from inside the man's coat. Gillian stared at the screen in disbelief at what she was seeing and hearing. She looked at William, eyes wide in shock and mouth agape.

"Are you telling me that a *suicide bomber* just nonchalantly walked into one of the most secure places in the United Kingdom, surrounded by armed police, S.O.1 agents and God knows who else, and strolls into the main chamber unchallenged before calmly setting off a bomb?" Even saying it back out loud, it sounded outlandish. Ridiculous even.

"I'm afraid so, Gillian," said William. "The other good news is that we have at least a month's worth of C.C.T.V. to look through before the explosion. Parliament Security kept a number of hard drives on site, in a metal fireproof cabinet. You know, to rotate usage for security. Anyway, those other hard drives have been recovered and they seem intact. We'll start going through them soon."

Gillian sat back in her chair, eyes still fixed to the screen. "Can you send me that evidence, as quick as you can please? I need to speak to Forensics. Good work William. Good work." She stood, still holding her coffee, and slowly made her way back to her office.

As she entered, she slowly closed the door behind her, and having walked around her desk, took a seat. She was still in disbelief about what she'd just learned. She slowly slid her half-eaten breakfast off the table into a bin on the floor and pulled her keyboard towards her and began to type up notes.

She intermittently stopped typing, trying to let what she'd seen sink in. The questions circling in her mind like a tornado. She knew this news would hit home hard to the public. How could this happen? There had been a number of terrorist attacks in and around London over the previous few years, on different targets. Security had been well-established and thankfully, there were less deaths than there could have been in those cases. But, how can someone just walk into the Houses of Parliament and detonate a bomb? No security. No errors. Completely covert.

She then picked up the phone and dialled. She waited a few seconds. "Hello – Forensics? This is D.C.I. Harper. I'm working on the Parliament case. I need to know if you've discovered any medals please, in or around the main chamber area." She waited for a few seconds. "You have? Brilliant. I'm on my way to you." She put down the phone, finished the last mouthful of coffee and left her office once more.

CHAPTER NINE
PIECING THE PUZZLE TOGETHER

New Scotland Yard - Forensics. 21st March - 10:27.

Gillian Harper arrived at Forensics. She flashed her badge on entry to a man dressed in a long, white coat carrying a clipboard. "I'm D.C.I. Harper, working the Parliament case," she said.

"Right over there, Detective Chief Inspector. Room three," said the man, pointing to a row of doors. She moved down the very plainly decorated corridor and entered the room numbered '3' and in it was table after table of what appeared to be burnt items. All recovered from Parliament and impeccably laid out on white table tops. Books, shoes, jewellery, watches, cufflinks, false teeth, glasses. All arranged in order of item. All numbered individually, with spotlights on the ceiling all pointing down on the items. Gillian closed the door quietly behind her and she walked passed item after item, looking at each one as she slowly walked towards a lady in a long, white coat at the other end of the room.

"Excuse me. I'm D.C.I. Harper. I called down a few minutes ago."

"Ah yes," replied the lady, "I'm Susan Pritchard, Forensic scientist. Welcome to Forensics." They shook hands. "So, I understand you're looking for medals? Is that right?" said Susan.

"Yes. It is very important I find a specific one."

Susan began to walk down one of the rows of tables, looking through a list on a clipboard. "I see. Okay, it looks like medals are numbered from '2,590' onwards, table forty-two. This way." Gillian followed behind. Susan walked slowly, checking tables on either side of her as she walked.

"So which specific medal were you looking for?" Susan asked.

"I'm actually not sure," came the reply.

"Then how do you know which one will be the one you need?" asked Susan.

"I'm hoping there are only a couple to look at?" she replied.

"I'm afraid not," said Susan with a chuckle, and stopped abruptly. Turning slightly to face a table, she pointed down onto it. "They start here D.C.I. Harper." Gillian looked down. There was row after row of medals. Each tarnished and black, each with the majority of ribbon burnt away. Each looking just like the other. She estimated that there were around fifty medals. Gillian sighed.

"How do we tell them apart?" Gillian said, slightly deflated.

"There is a way," said Susan. "We can clean them up. If luck is on our side, they should be individually named to the person that received it, provided they're not replica medals of course. There may even be a year attached to each one."

Gillian smiled. "Really? Fantastic. As of now, this has to be the main focus of the investigation. Can you please arrange for each of these to be cleaned up and send me a list of individuals names, if you find any? I can then cross-reference them to M.P.s and those that were meant to be there. Hopefully, only one of them will prove otherwise!"

New Scotland Yard. 21st March - 13:30.

D.C.I. Harper had called her team together again after lunch in the briefing room and showed them all the recovered video. "This is the latest information we have ladies and gentleman. Take it in! This was a suicide bomber. At the moment we don't know who he is. Who he represents. What his motives were. But we need to find out. Please note, he is wearing a medal and a beret." Gillian pointed to the screen, circling the medal and beret with her finger. "I have forensics cleaning up all the medals recovered from Parliament at the moment, so hopefully that should give us at least one lead. The press is baying for blood, so let's give them something plausible. Back to work people."

Mike Pierce and Rich Cope stood at the back of the room during the briefing. They looked at each other as the room was dismissed. Mike, looking worried, indicated with this head that they should go over to see Gillian. They walked slowly as the rest of the room emptied out.

"This is a major development," said Rich.

"Yes, it is," said Gillian. "And a major stroke of luck that the footage survived. We need to move fast. Once we have the names of those on the medals, I want you to go through the list. Match them off to anyone who was supposed to be there. That should leave us one name."

Mike and Rich nodded. "We're on it, Boss," said Mike, and they both turned to leave.

Back in her office, Gillian continued to collate all the information she had been given, and the video snippet and medal were the best hope of finding out what the hell happened three days ago. She looked up at the small TV mounted on her office wall. Sky News was playing but the volume was muted. The reporter on screen was reporting live from the ruins of Parliament. She turned the volume up a few notches so she could hear this breaking story.

"So, that Breaking News again. The Queen has spoken with the Deputy Prime Minister, Richard Baker and has asked him to form a new Government. He has accepted the role. He will now be taking on the title of Prime Minister of Great Britain and will spend the next few days building a new Cabinet, including presumably some of the remaining thirty-four M.P.s that survived from the previous Government. The investigation into what happened is still going on, with little news coming from the Metropolitan Police at present. We are assured, however, that they are working day and night to find out what happened." Gillian shook her head. "Here is what the new P.M. Richard Baker had to say earlier on." The camera changed to a view of the front door at No.10 Downing Street. There, stood at a small, wooden lectern with a black shield with the silver crest of No.10 Downing Street on it, was Richard Baker, still dressed all in black. His weary face showing that all of this was taking its toll on him physically and emotionally. His eyes were squinting with all of the camera flashes going off around him.

"It is with great reluctance that I accept this role as Prime Minister of Great Britain. I have assured Her Majesty the Queen that I undertake this role with a heavy heart but will strive to do my very best for her, for this country and for its people."

Gillian turned the volume off again and sighed. She placed her head between her hands, covering her eyes. She was tired. She rubbed her eyes. "Coffee," she exclaimed, as she got up from her desk and made her way to find some.

CHAPTER TEN
MISSING PIECES

Gillian Harper's home. 21st March - 19:45.

Gillian Harper had been home for little under half an hour and was pouring a glass of red wine when her mobile phone rang. It was a standard 'Old Phone' ringtone. She answered.

"Hello. D.C.I. Harper." The reply came.

"Hello, D.C.I. Harper. This is Susan Pritchard. We met earlier today, at Forensics. I'm sorry to bother you so late. I just thought you should know, we've managed to clean up the medals as best we could. We've managed to get a good number of the names, service numbers and years from them but not all I'm afraid. I've emailed them all to you." Gillian sighed.

"Thank you, Susan. I'll have a look now. Thanks for getting this to me so quickly." She hung up the phone and thought for a second, leaning on her kitchen worktop sipping her wine before moving to the living room, taking a laptop out from her shoulder bag and turning it on as she set it down on her coffee table, before taking a seat on her sofa.

At home, she looked completely different. She wore a matching pair of thick, cream, wool pyjamas. Her hair had been released from its pony tail and hung loose around her neck and shoulders. Her living room and her home was minimalistic. One sofa, one table, one television stand with T.V. A modern fireplace and a section of the wall with a number of white picture frames holding photographs of family and friends. Her living room was square, with no coving along the ceiling, and a single light hung from the centre. She spent most of her time either at work or out, and didn't consider filling her home with nick-nacks a luxury. She thought of it more a place to relax and sleep between working shifts. While her laptop was loading, she listened to faint, soft music coming from a small stereo system on the shelf. A few candles adorned her window sill and a tall, thin, standard lamp lit the room gently. She sat in contemplation for a moment listening to the music whilst waiting for her laptop to load, taking occasional sips from her wine. Slowly she leaned forwards and picked up her mobile. She selected a contact and pressed dial, whilst taking another sip of wine.

"Hello, Mike? Sorry to bother you. Look – Forensics have the information from those medals. I'm going to forward them on to you via email. Can you have a look tonight and see if there are any which seem obvious for any reason? Anything that jumps out at you." Mike replied.

"Of course. No problem. Is there something wrong?" he asked.

"No… not really. I just… haven't been sleeping well. I can't do any more tonight. I really have to get some sleep." replied Gillian.

"Yeah okay Boss, leave it with me. Get your head down and rest. I'll see you tomorrow."

Gillian hung up the phone. She hit a few keys on her laptop keyboard then closed the lid again. She finished her wine, placed the glass on the table, blew out the candles and went straight up to bed.

New Scotland Yard.22nd March - 0845.

It was raining. Hard. D.C.I. Harper walked into her office, soaked and placed her wet bag on her desk. She slipped her sodden coat off her shoulders and hung it on the back of her door, and placed her wet umbrella up against the wall leaning on a radiator. Despite the rain coat and umbrella, Gillian still had a couple of damp patches on her shoulders from the rain. She hadn't slept too well last night either. Although she got some sleep, it was restless which had given her a headache. She couldn't understand why it was happening. Normally she was a solid sleeper. Yes, this case was bigger than normal, but that shouldn't be causing her to lose sleep. She popped a couple of vitamin C tablets and two paracetamols in her mouth, and washed them down with a glass of water which was still standing on her desk from the day before. She hadn't spent any time looking at the email she was sent last night, and was anxious to find out what Mike had found. She looked out of her office door towards his desk. He wasn't there. Neither was Rich. She went back to her desk, sat down and opened her emails.

She sat and studied the e-mail. There was a list of about fifty names and service numbers, but she didn't have a clue what the numbers meant. She decided to bring it up at this morning's briefing in the hope that someone could explain the service numbers and how they related to the individuals. As she studied the e-mail, Mike and Rich knocked on the open door and walked in. "Morning Boss," they both said.

"Morning Mike, Rich."

Mike put a coffee cup from a local coffee shop down on Gillian's desk. "Thought you might need this," said Mike.

"White, no sugar right?"

She smiled and took hold of the coffee, and lifted it up to her nose, taking a big sniff. "Yep spot on guys, thanks. Ahh, I'm going to need this. I didn't sleep properly again last night. I don't know what's going on, but I really need a good night's sleep." She chuckled.

Mike and Rich looked at each other. "Well get that coffee down, I'm sure you'll feel better straight away," said Rich.

"Tell me about the list Mike. Did you get to take a look?" and she began to drink her coffee.

"I checked the list you sent me. And you were right. We've managed to pin most of the names on the medals to M.P.s of the House. Some were just dated. Mainly 1914-18 so we haven't counted those, as the man wearing it was clearly much younger. However, we found two which we couldn't find a match for. A Second World War medal, with a number that's before *any* of the missing Members of Parliament. We think this one was from a previous M.P. and may have been on a plaque or display of some kind, you know, in recognition? And a second."

Gillian leaned closer. "Go on," she said, sipping her coffee. Mike cleared his throat. "I think we have found our bomber."

Mike lay an A4 piece of paper down on Gillian's desk. On it was a face. The face of a man. She guessed middle-aged.

Gillian picked up the paper and studied it. "Who is he?" she asked. The face was thin, stony even. She estimated he must have been around fifty years old. He had short, clipped hair and had a number of small scars and pock-marks scattered across his face. He looked older than her estimated guess though, due to the wrinkles in his forehead and cheeks. He was unshaven, with at least a week's growth of stubble. His eyes seemed to stare holes directly into Gillian's brain. He looked rough, all right.

Mike replied, "This is Corporal 2453478 Stuart Jones. He was a Corporal in the Parachute Regiment between 1993 and 1997. He served two tours of Bosnia Herzegovina and one tour of Northern Ireland. He was awarded three medals. One United Nations for Bosnia, one NATO for Bosnia and one Northern Ireland medal. The medal that was found in Parliament was the Northern Ireland medal. No sign of the other two. We can't find much history on him. It appears since around 2009 he's been homeless, living on the streets of London. But let's just say, he wasn't an M.P. and this medal, or he, should not have been there."

Gillian thought for a moment. "We need to find out if the man in the video is definitely this Stuart Jones guy, and how and why he did this," she said.

As D.C.I. Harper, and D.S.s Pierce and Cope were talking in the office, the talking in the main office outside began to get louder. Gillian was trying to think but with the increasing noise levels in the office outside, found herself struggling to think straight. She put down the A4 piece of paper and walked out into the office. "What the hell is going on out here? I can hardly hear myself think!" she exclaimed.

One of the team turned around and faced Gillian. "D.C.I. Harper, you're going to want to see this." And he pointed towards the TV in the main office. Sky News was reporting more breaking news. She turned and speedily made her way back into her office, and turned the volume up on the TV in her room, and sat on the edge of her desk facing the TV. Mike and Rich also turned to view the television.

"Sky News has obtained a video from an anonymous source, of a man thought to have been the Parliament bomber. The video, uploaded to various social media sites as well as emailed directly to Sky News this morning at seven a.m. seems to be a confession by this man, forty-three-year-old Stuart Jones. Here in its entirety is the video." The clip began.

It opened on the face of Stuart Jones, the man on the piece of paper on D.C.I. Harper's desk. She picked up the paper and compared it – just to make sure. It was definitely him. The video only captured his head. The background was plain and impossible to locate, and Stuart Jones was looking down, almost remorseful. He began to speak.

CHAPTER ELEVEN
CONFESSION

"My name is Stuart Jones and I'm forty-three years old. I'm homeless and have been for… years. I forget how many. I'm originally from Hackney in London. I had a wife. I had a child, a son. I used to have a life. I was also in the Parachute Regiment and served in Northern Ireland. Since I left the forces, everything for me in civvy street went downhill. Due to Post Traumatic Stress, I began to drink. I couldn't hold down a steady job – I went through six I think, before I gave up. I became more and more depressed and I started to take it out on my family. Eventually they had enough and left, and I don't blame them."

"I couldn't afford to pay the bills on my own any more, and eventually I lost my house. I have been homeless since 2009 I think, and I've lived on the streets of London ever since, begging for food, for small change. For clothes. For shelter. For everything. For anything."

The pain on Stuart's face was obvious for all to see.

"My time in the forces were some of the best, but also worst days of my life. I faced things I never thought I would, and did things I never thought I could. But I did. For my Queen and for my country on the orders of politicians, we performed our duties to the letter. We followed orders. That's what we did."

Stuart's voice increased in volume. "Now those

politicians are trying to point the finger of blame at veterans who performed their duties over four decades ago, under *their* orders. One of those in the spotlight is my brother. Martin Jones. He's sixty-seven years old. He served in Northern Ireland in 1972 and followed orders. He always maintained he followed his orders to the letter. He returned fire when fired upon. He would have no reason to lie to me or his family and we all believe him. Now, living in residential care with no possessions and failing health, politicians and the Government think they can pin *Bloody Sunday* on him? He's lived a quiet, solitary life for thirty years. He's paid his taxes, he's obeyed the law. Now he is elderly and no longer has the strength to fight back against such accusations. The pain and suffering this is causing him? it's hard to put into words. He doesn't need it. He certainly doesn't deserve it. What he does deserve is the respect of Britain and its government!"

"So, to the British Government, I say this to you. Back in 2007, after hundreds of British soldiers fought and died in Northern Ireland, carrying out *your* orders, the British Government and the Prime Minister turned their backs on their own troops. The Prime Minister himself, at the time, made a pact with the very people trying to destroy us, by agreeing to forgive and forget all of the atrocities carried out by members of the I.R.A. These people were wanted for the murder of soldiers. But not just soldiers! Of women and children!"

Stuart's face began to sweat, showing signs of anger and hatred whilst his voice became louder and more powerful. His face was becoming contorted and glowing red and the rage flowing through him was evident.

"And not just murder! Torture! Arson! Bombing and blowing up! Knee-capping! How in any way is this legal? By turning your *own soldiers in* to be prosecuted and persecuted for doing their jobs carried out under *your* orders? Our own Government's Orders?"

"And why is this happening? Because Britain has lost her backbone. A nation with weak-minded fools as leaders. If something is wrong, there *must* be someone to blame! Because we can't have even one person whose feelings have been hurt! Because someone once said, 'Gee, British Soldiers opened fire on Bloody Sunday,' then someone must be held accountable? It was war! Things happen in war! And these things that happened were carried out under orders given by our government leaders. What is happening now, is that our leaders don't like 'history'. And this is their attempt to change and cover up their failings of the past."

Stuart paused and took a deep breath. He seemed to calm down.

"Yet history tells a blurred story. Where are the facts? Or do we not use facts any more before persecution can begin? Is it all about the witch-hunt? Having that one person to blame and throw rotten fruit at in the town square? Have we progressed as a people, or moved back to the dark ages? It was war. And this kind of thing happens in war."

Stuart began to get angry again.

"I know what my answer is! The answer is, the *Government* has to be held accountable! More so than any foot soldier ever should. Yet *they* point the finger at others, before others point the finger at *them!* Those politicians that were in office in 1972 now sit somewhere in retirement, with a huge pension paid for by us, by you and there's not a chance that any of them will ever be held accountable to actions of that day. How in any way is this right? How is any of this fair, I ask you?"

Stuart then paused. He looked around the room he was in, the tears welling up in his eyes. His anger dissipating and the sorrow welling inside of him. He closed his eyes tight and a single tear rolled down his cheek.

"And it's not just Northern Ireland that the Government need to be held to account for. It is the ongoing failings that continue to astound, every day. The number of veterans and ex-service personnel that continue to be affected by war, every minute of every day even after leaving the forces. They're left to their own devices to cope, with little or no help with mental health issues that they so desperately need. It's about the numbers of veterans and ex-service personnel that live on the streets when they leave the forces. It's about saying, 'Thank You,' to those who gave everything for Britain. For those who carried a rifle, so that those at home didn't have to. Sacrificed their time, their families, their limbs and even their lives. It's about supporting our veterans and troops to go back to a normal life. Why doesn't our country support our ex-forces and show them that we're thankful by housing them, by feeding them, by clothing them or by giving them free prescription drugs to help their daily battles? Battles they fight over and over, every day of every week, of every month, year after year. Or by offering free counselling and by supporting them in every way we can? They were willing to lay down their lives for this country. Many did. Surely the country should thank them for their sacrifice. Is that really too much to ask?"

"Finally, there are the rest of the country's problems which I really don't have time to get into in great detail, but let's just say this country is turning to shit! The N.H.S. is dying. Nurses, Police, Coast Guard, Air-Sea Rescue and Emergency Services pay should be more than footballers', for Christ sake! Armed Forces are getting smaller. Britain has stopped making and building things. It's all been shipped abroad. Old aged pensioners sit and die at home in the cold – hungry and alone. Their state pensions are atrocious. They can't afford to eat *and* warm their homes. They must choose which *luxury* to spend their monthly earnings on. Heating or food?"

"Child and family poverty in Britain has grown exponentially over the last few years. Almost three million children in this country are officially in 'poverty'. Why is the government allowing the working families of this country to go hungry and cold? Where is the sense in that? People work their entire lives giving money to the state, only for them to be ignored and abandoned when they're too old to feed any more money into the state. The fact that there are food banks set up by charities around the country *at all* to feed its own people is an *outrage*! This country is a disgrace. Now I'm no politician, but even I can see that this... *all* of this is wrong!"

Stuart's voice became louder once again. The anger becoming obvious. "Because of all of this, I have lost any and all respect for my Government. Those whose support was supposed to be unwavering to their military and its own people. I've lost respect for its leaders. Its decision makers. Its law makers. It has and continues to lose its way, and it needs a strong reminder about its purpose and what it's there to do, and who it's there to support. The people of Britain, and us ex-forces and *we've* had enough."

"So, there you have it. This is why I'm doing what I'm doing. I've served my country. I've paid the price for it. I've lost everything I hold dear, and more. I've lost money. Property. Self-respect. I've lost love and family. I've lost the good wishes of the British people who, instead of thanking me for my service, walk passed me, ignore me or spit on me and call me scum. The very people I carried a rifle for in the first place. And finally, I eventually lost myself."

Stuart's voice lowered to a calmer level.

"Before I do what I intend to do, I have a message for my ex-wife and son. I hope that one day you can see why I've done what I'm about to do. It's not about me. It's not about my brother. It's not about the PTSD. It's about what is right and what is wrong. It's about maintaining order and a Government that we can trust in, and a Government the people of Britain deserve."

"I could target just the Prime Minister, but if I did, another M.P. of the same mould would simply walk straight into her shoes. That is why I must eliminate *all* of Parliament. Britain needs new, fresh blood in power. We need new ideas, a new perspective. We need M.P.s from the *people* in power, not bred in upper class schools and colleges with silver spoons sticking out of their arses, who have no clue about living in poverty. Leaders who truly feel honoured to do what is expected of them, and who show the utmost respect for its people."

"I hope that one day son when you're old enough, you will understand that I had lost everything. I had nothing left to live for or lose. I was perfect for this job. I was never going to be coming home after this, and there was no way I'd ever survive in prison. I hope that one day when the right M.P.s and Prime Minister are in place, you will see that what I did was mercy, and needed to be done. And then, maybe one day you'll forgive me, for everything. That's all I ever wanted from both you and your mother. I'm just sorry I couldn't do it while you were around me. That's when I should have done it."

Stuart looked down. The sorrow and emotion etched on his face. Tears dripped from his nose.

"So, that's me!" Stuart wiped his eyes and straightened up. His face turned stony once more. "This is my confession. If everything goes according to plan, by the time you see this video my plan will have been a success. The British Government will be dead. The Queen will reign. It's now up to the people of Britain. Choose your leaders wisely. Choose who you give power to carefully. And if this ever happens again, then *fight! Fight* to take your country back!"

"God save the Queen, and God save Britain."

The video clip stopped and then cut back to the Sky News reporter. "Well, there you have it. That is the unedited clip we received this morning, as well as being distributed across social media UK wide. We've approached the London Metropolitan Police, but so far, they have declined to comment. We'll keep you updated with all the latest breaking news on this story."

CHAPTER TWELVE
END OF THE STORY?

Slowly, people in the office started to go back to their work, throwing unnerving and worried looks across the room in the direction of the D.C.I.'s office. D.C.I. Harper, still sat on the edge of her desk in her office raised the TV remote control and lowered the volume once more. She was in deep thought and took a seat behind her desk. She picked up the picture of Stuart Jones and stared at it for a few moments. D.S.s Pierce and Cope turned to face Gillian having already thrown glances between each other.

"So, case solved," said Mike.

"Looks like a lone nut who confessed, no less," said Rich.

They both stood, looking at Gillian who was still sat staring at the picture of Stuart Jones. The room was silent. D.S.s Pierce and Cope looked at each other wondering what she was doing. Then she spoke.

"*The people of Britain, and us ex-forces. We've had enough,*" she said.

"Come again?" said Mike.

"*The people of Britain, and us ex-forces. We've had enough,*" she repeated.

"I don't follow," said Rich.

Gillian looked up at the two D.S.s. "He said, 'The People of Britain, and *us* ex-forces. *We've* had enough.'" The two D.S.s continued to stare at Gillian. She looked at the paper again. "He wasn't working alone. He couldn't have been working alone. He must have had help. Forensics said that there were at least six devices in the chamber itself. How did he get them in there? One lone ex-soldier cannot get hold of that much military grade explosive and detonators, and then somehow get into the Houses of Parliament unseen to hide them. He was a Para. He was well-trained but he wasn't special forces. He can't have been working alone! He had inside help!"

Mike Pierce stepped forward, shaking his head. "Now hold on a minute Detective Chief Inspector, we don't know how much explosive he was carrying. The C.C.T.V. shows only that he wore a large, black coat. There could have been a ton of explosive under there. Surely that may have been enough to destroy the building?"

Rich then spoke. "Yeah. That's true," backing up Mike.

Gillian shook her head, her brain buzzing with questions and thought. "No, there's something not right here. Someone released that video to the press this morning. Now isn't it funny that it was released four days after the act itself? Why wasn't it released straight after the explosion? And why was it released on the same morning that we managed to get a name of this very suspect? No. Something is still going on in the background somewhere. He was working with someone, and that someone is working against us." She thought for a few seconds in silence.

"I'm going to get a coffee," said Mike. "Coming Rich? Do you want one Boss?" There was no response from Gillian. They both looked at each other, turned and walked out towards the canteen.

Gillian continued to think. Her eyes widened as a

realisation came over her.

"We have a leak," she whispered to herself. "We must have. There is no other explanation." She'd never experienced a feeling like it before, and she didn't like it.

She looked at her phone, examining it closely. She checked her laptop and desk phone. She had a look at the fire alarm sensor in her office for hidden cameras. She stood and looked out of the window, and scanned the buildings opposite and the ground below, before pulling closed the blinds. She then walked out into the main office and stood, looking at each member of the team from the back of the room. "If this is right, and we have a leak, then someone is drawing information from somewhere. It can't be from me. They can't be bugging me – I didn't even know this Stuart Jones until five minutes ago," she thought. She moved back into her office and went through a list of possibilities in her head and started taking notes in her notebook instead of on the computer. She waited in the office for Mike and Rich to return.

New Scotland Yard Canteen. 22nd March - 09:30.

Mike and Rich sat in the canteen sipping coffee, facing each other, their suit jackets slung on the back of their chairs. There were other police officers in the canteen too, but not many. They were all spread around the room, and not within ear shot of D.S.s Pierce and Cope. They both sat in silence, looking down into their cups of coffee.

Rich looked up from his cup, straight at Mike.

"Do you think she suspects?" he asked, quietly. Mike looked up from his cup.

"She's clever. She's trying to put the puzzle together. We

knew she would try," said Mike, scanning the room around him. "But as soon as she grasped onto the medal idea, I knew we had to leak the video. I told Stu *not* to wear that damn medal. But damn it, Stuart was stubborn as hell." Mike looked down at his coffee again. "You know this was the plan all along if she started to get too close. That's what Stuart signed up for. He knew it may come to this. He knew he may have to lay over the barbed wire for us." Rich nodded, looking around sheepishly. "We now have to make sure that she doesn't get us. Right?" said Mike. Rich nodded in agreement.

"Or anyone else," said Rich.

CHAPTER THIRTEEN
WORKING WITH THE ENEMY

New Scotland Yard. 22nd March 2019 - 10:00.

D.S.s Pierce and Cope returned to D.C.I. Harper's office. The door was closed, so they knocked. "Come in," came the reply. They entered.

"Mike, Rich. I think there are bigger things happening here." Gillian seemed flustered. "I think there has to be a leak or a mole, inside the Met."

Rich looked shocked. "What? How do you come to that conclusion?" he asked, his heart rate suddenly peaked.

"The release of the video to the press, ID'ing Stuart Jones, four days after the event. It's all very – neat and choreographed. Don't you think?" she asked. The pair looked back at Gillian and shrugged. "This could be bigger than all of us!" she exclaimed. "I can't find any bugging devices in my phones, or laptop but I don't think I'm the one that has been bugged as I only found out about Stuart Jones this morning. I've closed the blinds, just to be safe…"

Mike jumped in. "Whoa there Gillian. You're making this sound like some kind of grand conspiracy! Like we're being watched by everyone! This was one guy! *ONE*." Mike put his hands on Gillian's desk, leant forwards towards Gillian slightly, and lowered his voice, "Have you managed to get some rest? I mean real sleep?" asked Mike.

"No… no, not really," Gillian replied.

"Then why not take some time. Go home. Rest. Sleep. Come back tomorrow refreshed and with a clear head. Things may seem a bit clearer then," said Rich.

Gillian sighed. "We don't have time," she said through gritted teeth, appearing defeated.

"We can carry on digging into this Stuart Jones and questioning the other M.P.s whilst you're having down time. Don't worry – you taught us well." said Mike. Gillian, feeling deflated, nodded. She suddenly did feel exhausted. Maybe Mike was right. Maybe she wasn't seeing things or thinking clearly. She slowly stood, grabbed her bag, took her coat off the hook on the door, collected her umbrella and left the office, leaving her undrunk cup of coffee behind.

Mike and Rich looked at each other, still standing in Gillian's office. After a few moments, Mike spoke.

"We may need to increase the dose of Provigil in her coffee, Rich," said Mike.

"She's smart. She's starting to figure things out. But what affect will the increased dose have? It won't harm her will it?" asked Rich.

"No. It'll just help keep her awake longer, which will in turn make her tired and then she won't think straight. Look, I don't want her harmed. We've known her too long, and let's face it. She's one of us and she would have made a good Para. But if she knew we had a hand in this, she wouldn't think twice about locking us up and throwing away the key. That's the kind of person she is. Right – Wrong. Black – White. No in-between. We can't afford to let her into our secret. She's as straight as they come. And I'd rather keep her out of it altogether, but it wasn't my choice to bring her into this. It was a natural choice to let her lead this case. She's brilliant. But we need to be her equal and stop her investigation at every turn. You understand?" said Mike.

Rich nodded.

CHAPTER FOURTEEN
STRAIGHTENING OUT

D.C.I. Harper's Flat, London. 22nd March - 15:25.

It was mid-afternoon. Gillian had come home earlier in the day and taken a long hot bath. She'd tried to close her eyes in the afternoon on the sofa but snoozed restlessly. The sound of her living room clock seemed to increase whenever she closed her eyes. She tried to read a book, watch some TV, but found she couldn't concentrate on either. She then decided that something clearly wasn't right, so made a doctor's appointment for that very evening. She attended her local surgery at 17:30 and discussed the issue with her doctor. He took a blood sample and he'd said they'd run some tests, and prescribed her a few sleeping tablets, suggested she lay off any coffee, wine, cigarettes and any other stimulants, and that she could expect the results back within a couple of days.

Gillian had come home from the doctors', via a long walk passed the Thames. It was the last thing she wanted to do, but felt it might help clear her head. As she walked, the facts of the case were always there at the forefront of her mind. She kept replaying the confession from Stuart Jones over and over in her head. She felt a degree of sympathy for the man that blew up Parliament. There were a lot of things in the confession that Gillian agreed with, but she knew that the way Stuart Jones had handled the whole thing was wrong. She knew that despite her agreement on a number of subjects, that Stuart Jones had said, this was still murder. This was still terrorism. Just a new form of terrorism. One from inside, and she had to get answers before others followed suit and this turned into some kind of civil war.

When she did get home, all she could think about was the case. It was always there. How did the bomber get into the Houses of Parliament? How did he set up so many bombs? How could he get that much explosive? Her mind was fuzzy. She wanted to concentrate but couldn't. She decided to take one of her prescribed sleeping tablets and try to get some rest.

The Houses of Parliament, London. 23rd March - 09:35.

Having made a couple of phone calls earlier on in the morning, D.C.I. Harper arrived at the Houses of Parliament first thing. She had arranged to meet Susan Pritchard from Forensics on site. Gillian made her way through the cordon, having shown her I.D. to the armed police on site. The place was a mess. It was still cordoned off heavily and Gillian, having trouble parking her car anywhere near the crime scene, had to park back at the office at New Scotland Yard and walk the rest of the way. The place was still littered with a number of plain, white tents set up around the site, and people in white oversuits and masks still working the area. Armed police still patrolled the cordon around the edge of the devastation. The building resembled a deceased dinosaur. Its flesh withered away, leaving only the skeletal remains and ribs showing.

Gillian approached Susan. "Ah, good morning Detective Chief Inspector," said Susan, as Gillian approached her tent.

"Good morning Susan. Thanks for meeting me here at

short notice. I was hoping you'd help guide me through the crime scene and maybe give me your thoughts."

Susan, smiling replied, "Of course – follow me."

Susan led the way, via a path that had been cleared through the rubble. They manoeuvred under some more police cordon tape, passed a couple of armed policemen, and into where the Houses of Parliament used to stand.

"So, this is… sorry, *was* the main chamber." D.C.I. Harper couldn't make head nor tale of the site.

"Jesus, there's not much left," Gillian commented.

"On the contrary, there is a lot more left than you'd imagine," came the response from Susan.

She walked Gillian over to a hole in the ground and pointed down.

"Okay so this is where the bomber stood when the device exploded." Gillian looked down.

"Yes – it… looks like a hole," she commented.

Susan, not getting the joke, carried on. "You see this crater?" Susan knelt down and indicated around the circumference of the crater with her hand. "This is indicative of a blast above the surface blowing down, and in all directions. The blast moves down, carving out this crater section. The doors to the main chamber are… sorry, *were* here." Susan pointed in the direction of where the doors once stood. "Now, look over here." Susan moved across to another patch of ground. "Here, black scorched earth." Susan knelt again, pointing down. "A much smaller hole in the ground but still indicative of an explosive device, again above ground. This detonated lying on the surface. Maybe hidden, but physically sat on the ground. It was very strategically placed next to a supporting pillar."

Gillian seemed to be taking it in. "Okay, so what kind of explosive was this?" she asked.

"C-4. Plastic explosive. Definitely. The indications of the blast, the residue, the damage caused. No doubt about that. One hundred per cent," said Susan.

"What about the amount used? How much of it was used, and how did it get in here?" Gillian asked.

Susan thought for a moment. "I would estimate at *least* one hundred kilos. Each. That's about two hundred and twenty pounds," Gillian stared at Susan.

"Wait – so we're talking the weight of a human being, right? A person? That's massive!"

Susan nodded. "Yes, and that was just one. There were six in this room – not including whatever weight in C-4 that Stuart Jones was carrying."

Gillian's eyes opened wide. "*SIX*? How on God's earth did someone get six people's weight in C-4 into the Houses of Parliament without being seen? This is unfathomable!"

Susan shook her head. "No, not really. It's plastic explosive. So not detectable by metal detectors. And police don't routinely have sniffer dogs here at Parliament to search for this type of explosive. Plus, you can bring it in a little at a time. In the shape of, well, anything really. A bottle. A book. In a lunch bag. And then over time, keep adding it and adding it. You could probably manage it in a week or two, or if you have all the time in the world, a few months. Without being noticed, I mean."

Gillian, still shocked by the amount of C-4, asked her next question. "So, what can you tell me about the detonators?"

Susan replied, "So, we found traces of Tetryl. That's a chemical used in military grade detonators used by the British

Army and other military forces too. That indicates a basic C-4 and detonator set up. Not difficult."

Gillian nodded. "And any idea how it was detonated? Was it on a timer, or a trigger?" Susan nodded.

"We've found a number of 'plastic' shards scattered around the place. Whatever they were, there was a few of them. We're doing some tests on the plastic now to determine what it could have been used for, but I'm eighty per cent certain it's from some kind of remote receiver."

Gillian, listening intently, carried on with the questions. "So where did it come from?" Susan looked at Gillian over the upper rim of her glasses. "I would suggest asking the Military if they have misplaced a lot of C-4, detonators and remote devices in the last few weeks or months. If they haven't, it may be worth asking other countries if they've misplaced any, but I'd be more inclined to say it was obtained from within the U.K. just because of the amount used. It's not easy smuggling that amount of explosive into the country, or detonators unless under military guard or on military transport of some kind."

D.C.I. Harper left the scene. Her head was spinning with more questions than answers. But, she did notice she was feeling a little better. She felt she had a little more energy and was managing to think straight again, for now at least. She'd managed about six solid hours sleep during the night, which was the most she'd had in a number of days. She still couldn't figure out what had caused her to feel so lethargic in the first place. But, now that she was feeling like she was on the mend, she pressed on with her investigation and headed back to Scotland Yard.

CHAPTER FIFTEEN
LIFTING FOG

New Scotland Yard, London. 23rd March - 11:25.

Gillian sat at her desk. She looked around the room. It seemed gloomy. Darker than normal. She then remembered that she'd closed the blinds the day before. She remembered then, what had happened the day before. She got up and opened the blinds letting the natural light from outside back into her office. The sun was shining, which made her squint as the blinds opened. She sat back down and looked at the notes on her computer, then dialed a number from her desk phone, and waited.

"Ah – hello. Is that the Prime Minister? Hello, yes. This is D.C.I. Harper from the London Met. Apologies, we still have your mobile number on file. I really need to get hold of someone within the M.O.D. I understand the Defence Secretary was, well, unfortunately killed in the explosion. Have you appointed a replacement yet, or do you have the contact details for someone in the M.O.D. I can speak to please? As a matter of urgency, yes." She paused. "You have? Brilliant – yes please. Let me grab a pen." She shuffled around the top of her desk and found a pen in the top drawer, then grabbed her notebook from her coat pocket. "Okay, go ahead. Yes… yes… Okay. Yes, I have that. Do you have a name also? Brilliant. Thank you very much Prime Minister for your time." She hung up the phone then looked in the notebook she'd just written in. She closed it and placed it in an inside pocket of her jacket, before getting up and leaving the office.

She stood in the hall, looking into the main office. There was no sign of Mike or Rich. She took out her mobile phone, and dialed a number. She put the phone to her ear.

The call went straight to Mike's voicemail. She dialed another number. That call went straight to Rich's voicemail. "Where the bloody hell are they?" she asked herself. She walked into the office and asked out loud, "Has anyone seen D.S.s Pierce and Cope please?" Nobody seemed to know. She put her hands on her hips in disappointment. She turned and marched back into her office, shouting, "If anyone speaks to them, please get them to call me!" She closed the door and sat back in her seat.

No.10 Downing Street, London. 23rd March - 11:30.

The Prime Minister had just hung up the phone to D.C.I. Harper, and was sat looking at his phone. A worried look was on his face. He looked up across the desk at two men sat opposite him. "That was D.C.I. Harper. She wanted the number for an M.O.D. spokesperson. I had no choice but to give her it," he said.

The two men sat opposite, were D.S.s Pierce and Cope.

"Damn it!" said Mike. "She'll be no doubt trying to contact us too," turning on his phone. Rich did the same.

Richard Baker spoke up. "I thought you had this under control? She's sniffing around a little too closely. I've done my job by ensuring I'm clean. Don't let her get too close to me again. Guys, this conversation never happened, and you were never here. Get her off this path she's on otherwise this whole

89

plan goes up in smoke and we *all* get locked away for a very long time!"

Mike and Rich nodded. "We're on it." Mike replied.

Richard Baker sighed. "Have you managed to cover the tracks for the others?" he asked.

"Yes," said Rich. "We've fabricated their statements, and interviewed those not in the loop," he said.

Mike sat forwards. "As discussed, they'll never know the difference. They've all been into the station. Been captured on C.C.T.V. arriving and leaving. Their statements will get mixed in with the others and nobody will be any of the wiser," Mike said.

Richard Baker nodded. "Good. You're all good lads. You don't deserve any backlash from any of this. You were simply following orders." Mike and Rich both stood up and, having shaken Richard Baker by the hand, left via the rear exit to No.10 Downing Street.

They made their way to their car parked a few streets away. Mike dialed Gillian's number as they walked. "Hello? Sorry boss, did you try and ring? Yeah, we must have lost signal for a few moments," he lied. "Us? We're not far from the office – on the way in. We've just been for coffee. Want one?" hoping she'd say yes. "No? Okay then. See you shortly." Mike hung up the phone. "Shit. She sounds like she's composmentis. We need to get another dose or two of that Provigil into her system," said Mike. "Come on. She said she didn't want a coffee, but we'll get her one anyway. I'll say I just thought she could do with one. We'll get another dose in that and hopefully she'll be wide awake again by tonight."

CHAPTER SIXTEEN
DIGGING DEEPER

New Scotland Yard, London. 23rd March -14:37.

For the last few days, William Hacket had been working around the clock with his team, watching and re-watching C.C.T.V. from Parliament and the surrounding area.

D.C.I. Harper had decided to pay him another visit. "Hello William," she said as she entered the office.

"Ah, D.C.I. Harper. A pleasant surprise. What can I do for you?" he asked.

She had a quick look around, pulled a chair from another desk over to William and sat down next to him. She lent in closely. "William. We've worked together for a very long time. I trust you."

William looked away from his screen towards Gillian. "What's this about Gillian?" he asked, slightly confused.

"I believe we have a leak. Within the Met."

William's face changed from confused to a more surprised expression. "What's happened Gillian?" he asked.

She explained what had happened with the discovery of the medal, the identification of Stuart Jones and the anonymous leak of Stuart Jones' confession to the media.

William looked perplexed. "Hmmm, I think you may be on to something. This was a major incident, which didn't turn out to be a terrorist attack but was an attack from 'within' as it were. The last major incident of this magnitude was Guy Fawkes in 1605, apart from the fact it was foiled before any damage could be done. No attempt on Parliament has been tried since. And you don't commit this kind of act on a whim. It needs planning. Preparation. Execution. Reconnaissance. Practice. Timings. Whoever did this was a professional. I've read the dossier on Stuart Jones. Yes, he was once a highly-trained paratrooper. He served his country well. In his prime, he would have been a formidable character. But now, not so much. He'd been living rough for a number of years. He was malnourished. Had depression. Had PTSD. Was a heavy drinker. Probably hadn't had a good sleep in years. There is no way he did this on his own."

Gillian agreed. "So how about the C.C.T.V.? Have you managed to come up with anything?" she asked.

William slipped his glasses off his face. "My team and I have been over hundreds of hours' worth of C.C.T.V. from the outside of Parliament and, well, found nothing out of the ordinary. At all." Gillian sighed.

"What about inside?"

William placed his glasses back onto his face and turned to look back at the screens. "Actually, we're just about to begin the work on the inside C.C.T.V." he said.

"Excellent," exclaimed Gillian. She produced a piece of paper from her pocket. A bird's eye view of the Main Chamber within the Houses of Parliament. She'd marked six circles on the paper. "William, this is where forensics believe the explosives were detonated – these six locations. When you start reviewing the footage, please bear these six locations in mind. Whoever got the explosives into Parliament stashed them in these spots. Where the circles are used to be raised

M.P. benches. They may have been hidden under the benches or under the wooden floor supporting the benches."

William nodded as he took the sheet. He folded it and put it in his pocket. "I'll keep this with me," he said.

"William," said Gillian. "Please be careful. Only tell those you one hundred per cent trust. I don't want anything to happen to you."

William smiled. "I will Gillian. You take care. As soon as I have anything, I'll let you know," he said.

Gillian stood and wheeled the chair back to its desk and left the office.

New Scotland Yard, London. 23rd March - 15:00.

Gillian returned to her office. She made sure she told nobody about her visit to see William. She wanted to keep that conversation just between them. As she approached her office, she noticed the door was slightly ajar and shadows created by the sun moved inside.

She looked into the office. "Can I help you?" she said in a strong voice. D.S.s Pierce and Cope turned around, quickly.

"Geeze! You frightened the life outta me!" said Mike. Rich just laughed. This made Gillian smile. She entered and closed the door.

"Where have you been, Boss?" asked Rich.

This made Gillian slow her pace, just for a second, but she didn't answer. "How are you getting on guys?" she asked, as she took her seat behind the desk.

"Yeah, okay," Rich said. He placed a file with paperwork on her desk.

"What's this?" she asked.

"This is the complete history of all thirty-five surviving Members of Parliament, as requested," said Mike.

"Great, thanks. I'll start looking through this now," she said. She then noticed a coffee cup on her desk. It was steaming. "You guys got me a coffee? You two are the best," she exclaimed. Mike and Rich just smiled, before turning around and leaving the office.

Gillian opened the file whilst taking a sip from her hot cup of coffee. There in front of her was a pile of thirty-five dossiers. One for each M.P. She began to work her way through each of their histories.

New Scotland Yard, London. 23rd March - 16:30.

Gillian had worked in silence for the last hour and a half, just going through the dossiers, when her mobile phone rang in her pocket. She took it out and looked at the screen. 'Doctors' it read. She answered. "Hello, Gillian Harper."

A male voice answered. "Hello, Ms Harper, this is Dr. Fletcher. I've received your blood results back, and, well I need to speak to you. Urgently. Can you come in now?" he asked. Gillian was taken aback.

"Uh, well, yes I guess so. I'll be there in about twenty minutes?" she said. She hung up the phone and sat in silence for a moment. She then put all the documentation back into the file, put it into one of her desk drawers and locked the drawer. She then grabbed her bag and coat and left without telling anyone where she was going.

CHAPTER SEVENTEEN
SINISTER TWISTS

Dr. Fletcher's Medical Practice. 23rd March - 17:00.

Gillian arrived at the doctor's surgery. It was starting to get dark, so she pulled her car up to an empty spot and turned off her headlights, then the ignition. She sat for a moment. She was worried. For the short drive to the doctor's surgery, she had all kinds of things running through her mind with regard to her blood results. Some kind of infection? A disease perhaps? She didn't have time to be off work sick whilst investigating the biggest case Britain had seen in centuries. She got out of the car, fastened her coat and locked her car as she walked across the car park into the doctor's surgery.

Gillian entered and sat in the waiting area, flicking through a two-year-old copy of Perfect Living magazine. She wasn't really reading anything, just keeping her fingers busy as she waited.

"Gillian Harper, please," said the receptionist after a few minutes. Gillian stood, putting the magazine back onto the pile of other out-of-date magazines. "Room seven please," said the receptionist. Gillian made her way down the corridor and knocked on the door of room seven.

"Come in," came the reply.

She entered. "Ah, Ms. Harper. Thanks for coming so quickly," said Dr. Fletcher.

"It was no problem. So, what's with all the rush?" Gillian asked, as she took off her coat.

"Please, take a seat," said the doctor.

She did. Dr. Fletcher had a quick scan over the notes he had for Gillian, then turned to face her. "Have you been taking any kind of medication recently?" he asked.

Gillian, looking confused, replied, "No. The odd paracetamol and vitamin C, and of course the sleeping tablets you gave me. That's all."

Dr. Fletcher looked confused. He rubbed his chin. "Gillian, we found large quantities of various chemicals in your bloodstream including Modafinil, Lactose Monohydrate, Microcrystalline, Croscarmellose Sodium, Povidone and Magnesium Stearate. Now, I know all that might sound a little confusing but to put a simpler spin on it, I would say you'd been taking a stimulant drug to stay awake. Regularly. And a lot of it. Something like Provigil. Does that ring any bells?" Gillian was horrified.

"No – I haven't taken any tablets or medication except the ones I've just mentioned," she said.

"Then I would suggest that either you are *somehow* accidentally ingesting them or someone has been giving them to you," said the doctor.

Gillian was stunned. Nothing like this had ever happened to her before. "Like a spiked drink?" she suggested.

"Just like a spiked drink," he confirmed. "Although, of all the things to spike you with, I'm not sure why you'd be given Provigil or something similar. Its purpose is to keep you awake, not render you unconscious. It's like giving you a large number of energy drinks," he said.

Gillian sat and thought for a moment. "So this Provigil..

presumably it would disrupt my normal sleeping pattern, right?" The doctor nodded.

"Yes absolutely. And, if taken for long periods can inflict serious sleep deficiency issues in patients. You'd become nauseous. You mind would become over exhausted. This would cause side effects such as severe memory loss, concentration and problem-solving issues, anxiety may set in, sudden mood changes."

Gillian just sat, stunned. Everything the doctor was saying seemed to make sense to her. It would certainly explain how she had been feeling over the last few days.

"So, how would something like this be administered?" asked Gillian. The doctor replied with the answer she was dreading to hear.

"Well, a number of ways, but primarily ingested. So, if not taken directly, can be added to a drink or food for example. As you said earlier - spiked."

As Gillian left the surgery her mind was racing. Was someone intentionally giving her these drugs, and if so – why? Or better yet, how? She walked to her car slowly, unlocked it and threw her handbag across to the passenger seat, before climbing in. She sat for a moment, looking around. Was she being followed? Or watched? Why was this interest in her? What had she done to warrant being pinpointed? And how were they getting the drugs into her? Quickly, she started the car, turned on her lights and left the carpark at speed. She just wanted to get home, lock the doors and think.

D.C.I. Fletchers home. 23rd March - 17:50.

She arrived home soon after. Quickly she grabbed her bag from the passenger seat, climbed out of the car, closed the door and locked the car. She moved quickly, somewhere between a fast walk and a jog to get to her door, head down. She fumbled for her keys and shook slightly, trying to get the key into her door lock, breathing fast. Once inside, she slammed the door and locked it. Even putting the chain over the door; something she had never done before. She turned and leaned up against the front door and burst into tears. She stood there, sobbing for a few moments before regaining her composure. She walked down her hall to the living room, where she turned on her tall, standard lamp, slipped off her coat and dumped her bag on the sofa. She picked up a small remote control and pressed play. A low level of classical music began to play from her small, stylish stereo system which was in the corner of her living room. She headed for the kitchen and poured herself a large red wine, hesitating when putting the bottle down on the kitchen worktop, only to return and take the rest of the bottle with her. Then she returned to the living room where she wiped her eyes and sat for some time, thinking about how this was getting into her system, letting the wine and the music seep into her soul in an attempt to calm her mood.

As she sat, contemplating things, she decided that the only way to pursue this case was to change her mentality. She wiped her eyes again, pulled a tissue from a nearby box and blew her nose, then took another stiff drink of wine. "I've been doing this job for twelve years," she thought. "I've had threats against my life before but only from the likes of drunken yobs and small-time crooks. Nothing like this." In reality, she was only just beginning to realise how big this case was. Was she facing a case which was the pure result of a lone nut, or was this bigger? Way bigger? Could it be a secret society or a collusion of Governments and States, like Russia or China?

She didn't know. What she did know however, was that she was good, strike that - *very* good at her job. And she had to change her mentality to outwit whatever or whoever was behind all this.

She knew that there was someone on the inside who couldn't be trusted, but she didn't know who. The only way to outwit them, she thought, was to assume that *everyone* was working against her. She had to keep what she found to herself and only involve those she absolutely needed to in order to solve this case.

Her job was everything to her. She had no immediate family, no husband or children. She'd spent the majority of her life working for the Met and had loved every minute of it. She had no plans for the future in regards raising a family, and never really considered the possibility of moving jobs. She'd spent the best years of her life at the Met and she was damned if anyone was going to get the better of her on this case, or any other. And, since she'd found out that someone was administering her some kind of drugs, presumably to mute her ability to investigate properly, this was now becoming personal. Enough, she thought. It's time to blow this case wide open.

CHAPTER EIGHTEEN
FACING THE TRUTH

New Scotland Yard. 24th March - 08:00.

Gillian arrived at work early. She poured herself a cup of coffee and settled down into her office. She was about to pull the file from her locked drawer and begin going through the M.P.s information in front of her again, when she noticed that her drawer wasn't actually locked. She paused for a moment, as she looked at the drawer. She was sure she locked it. She tried her key to make sure the lock wasn't broken. It wasn't. This immediately arose suspicion, but all the files were still in her drawer and nothing was missing. She had managed a good night's sleep and felt refreshed. She also felt she had a new purpose and continued her investigation with new vigor, and as she'd found out someone was trying to impair the investigation with some kind of drug, she felt she was actually on the front foot for a change.

She was looking for anything that could link these M.P.s to Stuart Jones somehow. She compared ages. Hometowns. Interests. Political views. Nothing seemed to be working. She couldn't find anything that would even be considered a faint link, let alone a strong one. Then, by chance, she was looking through the dossier of one M.P. Martin Holdsworth, a surviving Labour M.P., when she noticed an anomaly in the dossier. It wasn't a big issue, but each page was numbered. In this particular dossier there appeared to be a page missing. The pages in order, jumped from page five to page seven. First, she thought it might be a typo. So, she moved onto another dossier. Claire White – Liberal Democrat. This one had a page six. This particular page held information about previous job history. In Claire White's case, she was working in administration for a number of years after college, many years beforehand. Strange, thought Gillian. She carried on going through all the dossiers until eventually, she had a pile of those with a page six, and those without. The pile of dossiers without a page six, totaled sixteen files.

New Scotland Yard. 24th March - 09:10.

Gillian was sat contemplating the two piles of dossiers when there was a knock at the door. "Come in," she said.

In walked D.S.'s Pierce and Cope. "Morning Boss," Mike said.

"How was your night?" asked Rich.

Gillian hesitated for a second. "It was okay I guess. Had a glass of wine and an early night. I did find something out last night which was weird though," she said, preparing to tell them about her visit to the doctor. However, just as she was about to, Mike placed a fresh steaming cup of take-out coffee onto her desk right in front of her. She stared at the cup of coffee, before a flush of realisation came right over her.

"Oh yeah, what was that then Boss?" asked Mike.

Gillian stared at the cup, whilst snippets of the doctor's conversation flashed across her memory. 'Just like a spiked drink,' she heard her doctor's voice repeat in her head.

"Boss?" asked Mike. "Are you okay? You seem

preoccupied," he said.

Gillian suddenly snapped out of it. "Oh – yeah sorry. I was just thinking about something." Mike and Rich smiled.

"So, what were you saying? Finding out something strange?" asked Rich.

"Oh – I, um, I found that I can't open a bottle of red wine without finishing the whole bottle." said Gillian, thinking quickly and making it up on the spot.

The two D.S.s laughed. "Fair enough." said Mike.

They were just about to leave the office, when Mike noticed the two piles of dossiers. He looked straight at Rich and indicated down to the files. Rich looked too.

"What's with the piles of dossiers, boss? You found something?" asked Rich.

"Oh – I'm trying to find any commonality between any of these and Stuart Jones. I'm pulling at straws really. I haven't found anything concrete yet. But I'm still looking," she said, as she pulled the two piles together again. Both Mike and Rich nodded before leaving the office and walking out.

Gillian sat back in her chair and stared at the coffee. She didn't want to believe that either Mike or Rich, or indeed both had anything to do with her being drugged. But she couldn't think of any other way it was possible. There was only one way to find out. She put the dossiers away again, locked the drawer, grabbed her coffee and headed out the door.

Scotland Yard, Forensics. 24th March - 09:30.

Gillian, making sure nobody including Rich and Mike saw her leave, marched with a rigorous vigor and arrived at Forensics. She headed straight for Susan Pritchard's office. Her head was a blur. She knew what she had to do, but didn't want to believe what the likely outcome of the following meeting could potentially bring. She knocked. "Hello?" came the reply.

Gillian entered. "Hello Susan," she said and closed the door behind her, scanning the room to make sure they weren't in ear shot of others nearby. "I need a favour," Gillian said quietly.

"Okay, I'll do what I can. How can I help?" Susan asked, a puzzled look on her face. Gillian leant over the desk towards Susan and placed her coffee onto the desk. Sliding it slowly towards Susan, Gillian said, "I need you to test this please. Straight away. For any strange substances or drugs that shouldn't really be in coffee." Susan looked at Gillian with a perplexed look on her face.

"Are you sure?" she asked with a disbelieving smile on her face.

"Deadly sure!" she replied. Susan's smile disappeared. "And the results come to me. And me alone!" Gillian stressed, as she continued to scan the room around Susan.

"Of course, I can get some results back to you this afternoon."

"Thanks Susan. This is between you and me only. Nobody else. Okay?" Susan nodded. Gillian turned and left the office, closing the door behind her, and headed back to her office making sure nobody saw her.

New Scotland Yard. 24th March - 09:45.

Back in her office, Gillian sat behind her desk and drew a large breath. She closed her eyes to think for a moment, before picking up her phone to make a call. "Hello, is that records? This is D.C.I. Harper. I'd like a copy of each of the surviving thirty-five M.P.s' statements please from the Parliament blast. Yes, I'm aware my team already have copies, but I need another copy for my own records. You can? Great. I'll be down shortly," and she hung up the phone. She knew her team had copies of the statements, but as she didn't know who else was working against her, she couldn't trust any of her team not to pass on the vital information she so desperately needed. She decided to look at all the evidence herself. She left her office once more and headed down to records. She waited around whilst the copies were printed and after collecting them, swiftly went straight back to her office having placed the files in her bag.

Gillian took the pile of sixteen dossiers that had page six missing, and collated the statements from those same sixteen M.P.s. She sat and looked through each one. Each statement was as she would expect. Thorough. Well-executed. Every second accounted for. In short, perfect statements. In fact, they were *too* good. She knew human error occurred often and not one of these statements had any kind of obvious errors. No spelling mistakes, no doubt shed on any of the statements, every second of every minute accounted for, nothing. This was unusual. She looked through some of the other statements. Those did have some spelling errors, questions about timings, conflicting information. But the original sixteen – nothing. The fact that they were all perfect was suspicious. She took a note of the sixteen M.P.s names and details in her own little notebook, then mixed all the dossiers up again. She put them back into her lockable drawer, made sure the drawer was locked and placed the copied statements into her bag. She didn't want to leave them in the office and arouse suspicion that she was onto something and to help back that up, she called a team brief.

CHAPTER NINETEEN
PLAYING THE PLAYERS

New Scotland Yard Briefing Room. 24th March - 10:30.

Gillian arrived in the briefing room and the whole team were already there except D.S.s Pierce and Cope. The team sat on chairs facing the front of the room, where Gillian stood once again leaning up against the desk, arms crossed. This time, she'd invited Susan Pritchard and William Hacket to the brief. She wanted to make sure that she was being seen to be doing all she could and utilising all available bodies in this investigation, to anyone within the team who wasn't fully focused on getting the result she wanted.

"Morning people. I'd like to know from each of you where we are with this investigation so far please. Since the last brief where we saw the footage of Stuart Jones entering the main chamber of the Houses of Parliament, and following on from his confession, what have you all managed to uncover?" The room remained silent. As Gillian slowly paced the floor in front of the group, her head bowed and arms firmly crossed, D.S.s Peirce and Cope slipped in quietly to the back of the room, which Gillian noticed.

Gillian waited. "Anything?" she asked. There was still no response. "Okay. First of all, have we found any anomalies in any of the statements from the thirty-five?" Gillian asked.

"No Boss," came the response from a man sat near the

front. He was leaning back, one leg crossed over the other and his hands held together on his knee. "No anomalies at all. All the statements check out," he said, giving a shrug of his shoulders.

"Hmm. Okay. What about external C.C.T.V.? Anything there?" Gillian asked. She already knew the answer, having gone to see William the day before, but wanted the whole team to hear the answer.

"No, nothing new on face recognition or additional suspects. No suspect packages or mail delivered. Nothing out of the ordinary going in or out for at least a month leading up to the explosion," William replied.

"Forensics. Anything new there please?" Gillian asked.

Susan was at the back of the room, sat on a small table. "Yes. The black shards of plastic we found scattered around the room were absolutely from some kind of radio-receiving devices. So, we now know that the bombs were detonated remotely. We can say that with around eighty-five per cent accuracy." she said. "We also found evidence of a remote detonator within the rubble which we suspect was carried by Stuart Jones, and triggered just after he walked into the main chamber. I strongly believe that when Stuart pressed the trigger, or button, or whatever it was, it triggered the other devices at exactly the same time." Gillian stopped pacing and thought for a moment.

"Thank you, Susan, excellent news. Can you work on finding out the make and model of the transmitter and receivers please? Well done on confirming that. At least we have something to go on." Susan smiled and nodded. D.S.s Pierce and Cope, both leaning up against the back wall with their arms crossed, looked at Susan with stony faces.

Gillian paced in front of the team once more. "So, apart from that we have nothing new?" she asked. She stopped pacing. "People – the whole world is watching this investigation. The Press are baying for blood. We need more! I know you're all trying your best, but we need to dig deeper people. We don't want to look like fools in front of the world's press, not to mention that we owe three hundred and ninety-eight families an explanation."

"Actually, it's now four hundred and two families boss. Over the last few days, four more have died from their injuries in hospital," came the sheepish response from a young, female team member sat amongst the group. Gillian scanned the faces in the room. All of the team seated seemed disappointed. She was hoping one or two would make themselves a bit more obvious by not showing any emotion or by giving away any little 'tell-tale' signs. But they didn't. The only two that flagged up in Gillian's test, were D.S.s Pierce and Cope. They just stared at Gillian.

"Okay people, thanks for the updates. Back to work please." And the room slowly and silently emptied.

Gillian was now sure in herself that no others within the team were working against her, apart from D.S.s Peirce and Cope. In a way she felt relieved, but also at the same time felt betrayed by the pair of them. But, she couldn't be absolutely sure until the forensic results came back from her coffee. She prayed that they were negative results, but couldn't think of anyone else that could be administering these drugs.

William approached Gillian in her office after the brief. He closed the door behind him. "What was that all about, Gillian?" he asked, looking perplexed.

"William, I think I now know who is working with me and

who is working against me. And that little show in there just confirmed a few facts for me," Gillian said.

William sighed. "You were on a mole hunt?" he asked.

"Yes. In a roundabout kind of way," she said, leaning back in her chair. William nodded.

"I see. Gillian, stay safe. That's all I ask," William said.

Gillian smiled, "I will," she replied. "Before you go, William. I have a list of M.P.s here. I'd like you to keep particular close attention to them when you review the internal C.C.T.V. footage of the chamber for the few weeks leading up to the explosion." Gillian produced her pocket book. She tore out a page from her notebook and handed William the piece of paper. "Please keep this safe. This is between you and me only," Gillian said.

William took the page and looked at it. "I will," he said. "But there are a lot of names here. Are there any you want me to concentrate more on than any others?" William asked.

"No. Any and *all* of them," she said.

William scratched his head. "Okay, but it may take some time," he replied, folding the paper and placing it into his pocket.

"Thanks William," said Gillian, as William turned and left the office.

New Scotland Yard. 24th March - 12:00.

Gillian sat at her desk and took her notebook out. She opened it and found the note she took from Richard Baker and the contact details for a spokesperson at the M.O.D. She'd written 'Lieutenant Colonel Fitzpatrick' and a telephone number. She placed the notebook onto the desk, picked up her desk phone and dialed the number. It rang a couple of times before being answered.

"Hello M.O.D. Liaison, Lieutenant Colonel Fitzpatrick speaking."

Gillian took a breath. "Hello Lieutenant Colonel Fitzpatrick. This is D.C.I. Harper from the London Metropolitan Police Service. I'm wondering if I can speak to whoever would be covering the Minister for Defence position. I'm conducting the investigation into the blast at Parliament and I was wondering if they could spare me a few minutes, please?" she said. There was silence for a moment.

"I can help with any query you may have in the absence of a Minister for Defence. How exactly can I help you, D.C.I. Harper?" he asked.

"Well, it appears from forensic examination that the explosive used in the blast was caused by C-4. And a lot of it. Also, there were traces of Tetryl found at the scene, as used in military grade detonators, as well as fragments from what we believe is a remote, detonating device. From what we can gather, there was over half a ton of C-4 used, possibly more. I'm wondering if there have been any reports of lost or misplaced C-4 or detonators over the last couple of months from within any of the forces, please?" Again, there was silence for a moment.

"D.C.I. Harper, when the Army go out on exercise and need to practice their trade, soldiers will sign out a certain amount of C-4 and detonators. Once the exercise is over, if they still have an excess of C-4, they do not return it. They detonate it. Also, at the end of every exercise, each and every service person that has handled explosives and ammunition must make a declaration that they have used it all up, and are not taking any explosives or ammunition away from the training area. It is possible that someone making this declaration wasn't being completely truthful and took an amount. There have been no reports of any thefts, or reports of anyone found taking any C-4 or detonators without authorisation and we do not have the time nor the personnel to search each and every soldier we train, as and when they leave the training area."

Gillian rubbed her eyes with one hand, whilst holding the phone to her ear with the other. This wasn't exactly the help she envisaged. "That's all I needed to know, thank you for your time Lieutenant Colonel." And with that, the conversation was over and she hung up the phone.

CHAPTER TWENTY
POSITIONING THE PIECES

New Scotland Yard. 24th March – 14.24.

Gillian was walking down a busy London street. She was returning to Scotland Yard from a sandwich shop, sandwich in hand and a cup of coffee, when her mobile phone rang. She rolled her eyes, stopped and placed her coffee down on a wall. She pulled her phone from her pocket and looked at the screen. 'Susan Pritchard' it read. She answered. "Hello. D.C.I. Harper."

"Ah, hello Gillian. Susan here," came the reply. "I have some news for you, regarding…" before she could finish, Gillian interrupted.

"Don't say any more, Susan. I don't know how secure my line is. I'm five minutes away. I'll be there shortly," Gillian said.

"Oh… Okay. See you in a moment," Susan replied. Gillian hung up the phone. She suddenly began to feel very nervous. She shuffled her phone back into her pocket, picked up her coffee and carried on walking back towards the Yard, her pace now more urgent.

New Scotland Yard, Forensics. 24th March - 14:35.

Gillian entered the Forensics department and headed straight for Susan's office, sandwich and coffee still in hand. Balancing her coffee on the hand carrying her sandwich, she knocked.

"Come in, come in," came the reply.

Gillian entered the office. "Hello Susan. Sorry for cutting you off mid-sentence but at the moment, I'm not sure who I can trust and who is listening in."

Susan grimaced. "I don't blame you, having seen the results from the coffee you gave me this morning," Susan replied.

Gillian was hoping in her heart of hearts that nothing would be found, but by the sound of what Susan was about to tell her, she knew it was bad news. Susan ushered Gillian to a quiet area of the room, where she leant into Gillian slightly and began to speak softly.

"Unfortunately, you were right Gillian. In the coffee you gave me, I found traces of various chemicals. Mostly made up I believe, to be some kind of stimulant." Susan looked down and read from a white A4 piece of paper which had the results printed on it.

Gillian sighed. She looked down at the floor and having placed her lunch on a nearby table, rubbed her eyes. "Yeah, I thought you might. I was hoping you wouldn't find anything but... something told me you would," Gillian said wearily.

Susan stood and faced Gillian. "What is going on here, Gillian?" she asked in a concerned way, rubbing Gillian's arm.

Gillian looked up at Susan. "There are a number of people working against me on this case. I don't know why yet, but I will find out," said Gillian. "Please do not mention this to anybody else. This is between you and me. Please," begged Gillian.

"Of course, of course," said Susan.

"Can I take this report?" asked Gillian, reaching out to take the piece of A4 paper.

"Yes, by all means. Take it," said Susan, handing it over.

Gillian folded the report and put it into her pocket. "Thanks Susan. I have a feeling this will become very handy once this case progresses," she said, as she collected her lunch and turned to leave the room.

Gillian walked back to her office. Continually scanning people as she walked. She was looking for signs, anything that might suggest that they were keeping tabs on her. Her anxiety was building, as was her paranoia. She felt eyes on her whenever she moved around, but kept her cool very well. She reached her office and closed the door.

Having removed her coat, Gillian sat at her desk. She removed the copies of the M.P.s statements from her bag and placed the forensic drug report with them. She then placed them in a large, A4, brown envelope and then placed that back into a zip-sealed pocket of her bag. She had decided that keeping this evidence separate was paramount. The last thing she wanted, especially if people were sniffing around her office, was to leave this damning evidence lying round for someone to find and dispose of. She'd decided to keep the evidence in her own safe – at home. Gillian's new plan was to keep D.S.s Pierce and Cope busy. To make sure they didn't feed her any more pills or drugs and to make sure they were kept as far away from her, for as long as possible to enable Gillian to complete her investigation unhindered. She decided to do that, right from the off.

CHAPTER TWENTY-ONE
EXECUTION

New Scotland Yard. 24th March - 16:22.

Gillian had called D.S. Pierce on his mobile and asked if they could both come in for a chat. Gillian waited in her office. She'd placed all the dossiers on her desk in a big pile and picked the first one off the top to look through whilst she waited. Then came the knock on her door. "Come in," she said. In walked both Mike and Rich.

"Afternoon, Boss," said Rich.

"Ah, thanks for coming guys. I just wanted a quick catch up. Just to see where we were with the investigation."

Mike closed the door and they both sat down opposite Gillian at her desk. Mike handed over a coffee. "Got this for you, Boss, on the way in."

Gillian looked at it. "Oh, thanks Mike. I'm... still not sleeping right," she lied. "This should help wake me up." She took the smallest of sips, pretending to take a larger mouthful. "So, what have you two got to report?" she asked, still holding onto the coffee.

Mike replied. "So, we've been going through statements from the M.P.s trying to find any links or ties."

Gillian stared at the pair of them. "And?" she asked.

"Well, nothing yet Boss," said Rich.

"So, what's your plan?" she asked the pair of them.

They looked at each other. "Continue to investigate the evidence we have, Boss. Until we have any further evidence, we can't do a lot more," said Mike.

"Hmm," nodded Gillian. "We need to progress this case quickly," Gillian said. "We've already got some of the team going through those statements, so no point doubling up the work effort. I'd like you two to spend the next two days on site, at Parliament. I want you hanging over the shoulders of the forensics guys and as soon as they find anything, I want to know about it," Gillian said.

Mike and Rich looked at each other again. "Boss…" said Mike. "We could just place a bobby there to do that. We could be used to do more important work."

This was exactly Gillian's plan. "Yeah, I know. But this case is huge. I won't trust a bobby to do that. You know me, and you know how badly I need the evidence. That's why I want to send my top two guys to oversee and monitor the work on the ground. Can you do that for me?" she asked. Mike and Rich shrugged.

"Yeah… I guess so," said Mike. Rich nodded too.

"Great. Thanks guys. Remember. If you see or hear anything, I want to know about it first," Gillian reiterated.

"Okay Boss," said Rich. They both stood and left the office, glancing at each other.

Gillian sighed a big sigh of relief. She was hoping this would keep those two out of the way for a couple of days at least. She then looked at the coffee in her hand. "I know where you're going," she thought, and took it straight to the ladies' toilet and poured it down the sink, making sure she took the empty cup back to her office and leaving it on her desk for continuity, just in case either Mike or Rich decided to pay her office a visit again overnight. She also decided to lay a little trap by putting a single hair from her head between two strips of sellotape on her lockable drawer, between the locked drawer and the one below. She knew that if that hair was broken tomorrow, that someone had indeed been through her desk.

D.C.I. Harper's home. 24th March - 18:40.

Gillian, having returned home from work, hung her coat on the hanger by the front door. She dropped her bag on her wooden floor underneath the hanging coat, and slouch- shouldered, turned to enter her living room. Suddenly she stopped and returned moments later, having remembered the important documents held within the bag. She bent down and having retrieved the envelope containing the missing statement sheets, and the coffee report from Susan Pritchard, made her way into her second bedroom-come office space. She opened a wardrobe and cleared some shoes from the bottom of it, revealing a small metal safe. It was a plain safe, dull silver in colour with a small screen and digits 1 to 0 on the front. She entered her four-digit code. 4... 1... 7... 2... and waited. A moment later the safe gave a small 'beep' followed by a small clicking sound. The door then opened itself, only a short way. Just enough to pull it open the rest of the way with a finger. As the safe opened, it revealed its contents, which wasn't much. A passport, some documents and a small jewellery box. Gillian pushed the brown envelope into the safe. It was a pretty tight fit, so she had to bend it slightly to make sure it fit in properly. Once inside, she closed the door again. Once closed, the safe gave another short 'beep' of a lower tone than before, followed by a short succession of clicks once again. It was locked.

She shuffled the shoes back in position in front of the safe, then closed the wardrobe door once again.

CHAPTER TWENTY-TWO
CLOSING THE NET

D.C.I. Harper's home. 25th March - 07:22.

Gillian had only been out of bed about fifteen minutes and had just come out of the shower, when she heard her mobile phone ring. She dashed through to her bedroom from the bathroom, wrapped in a plain pale blue towel and still dripping water as she ran and picked it up from the bedside table. The number was showing as withheld. She hesitated a moment but answered it.

"Hello?" she said.

"D.C.I. Harper. This is William Hacket. I'm very sorry to disturb you so early but I wanted to ask you to come to my office the moment you get in please," he asked, sounding desperate.

"Good morning William. Well yes, of course. That's fine," Gillian stated.

"It is of the utmost importance." he stated sternly.

"I'll be there about eight," she said. Gillian ended the call there. She looked at her phone for a second, pondering, before realising that she was still dripping water all over her polished, wooden bedroom floor.

"Shit," she exclaimed, before throwing the phone onto the bed and running back into the bathroom to finish drying off.

Gillian entered Scotland Yard and flashed her I.D. as she walked passed security. She walked to the lift but stopped. Just in case she was being watched, she decided to take the stairs instead, and took a different route to see William Hacket. She didn't want to be spotted by any of her team. She climbed the few flights of stairs, entered the floor and knocked on William's office door. "Enter," came the reply. Gillian entered, and slipped off her coat and bag.

"Morning William. What do you have for me?" she said, as she pulled up a chair and sat next to William.

"Morning Gillian. I'm sorry for the early call, but thought you'd want to know about this straight away. I haven't told anybody else yet. I guessed that's how you'd prefer it?" he asked.

Gillian nodded. "Thanks William, that's exactly how I'd prefer it," she said.

William turned to his screen. On his desk lay a keyboard, mouse, pens and various bits of paperwork. He shuffled around on his desk, clearing space and making room for the mouse.

"So, I've been going through the C.C.T.V. from within the chamber for the immediate two weeks leading up to the explosion. I've been paying particular attention to the list of individuals you gave to me. Now, I've highlighted these individuals with colours, and what I've been able to do is track those individuals more easily amongst the crowds of other M.P.s." William showed Gillian a bird's eye view of the chamber on the screen. On the diagram were sixteen differently coloured spots, dotted around various locations of

118

the chamber. "I'm now going to start moving through the days leading up to the explosion. Keep your eyes on the coloured dots and see if you can make out a pattern, okay?" said William. Gillian nodded. William clicked through the fourteen days. Each day, the coloured dots moved around the room. When the sequence of slides was finished, William turned to Gillian. "Did you see a pattern?" he asked.

Gillian shook her head. "No, not really." she said.

William nodded. "Okay, well let's make this a little easier," he said. He clicked on his mouse a couple of times and this time, six circles appeared, overlayed on top of the chamber. "So, now I've added the locations of the six individual explosive devices," he said.

Gillian nodded, still transfixed on the screen. William began the sequence again. This time she kept an eye on the circled locations as the colour sequences changed.

"How about now?" asked William, once the sequence of fourteen days was complete again.

"The colours changed all the time," she said, shaking her head.

William nodded. "Exactly," he said. "The strange thing is, most of those sixteen M.P.s occupied those six locations at one point or another. Always – except one. Richard Baker. As Deputy Prime Minister, he sat in the same place each day, next to Patricia Kaine. There were hundreds of people in that room, every day. Yet only those fifteen people occupied those six places over the course of the two weeks leading up to the explosion. That in itself is strange, is it not?" William said.

Gillian, sitting back in her chair, looked at William. "Are you saying that any one of those 15 could be a suspect?" she asked.

William shook his head. "No. I would suggest that *ALL* fifteen are suspects." he replied. Gillian thought for a moment.

"All those M.P.s had pages missing in their dossiers. Every one of them. I need to find out what information is on those pages, and why they are so important." Gillian stood up. "I'm sorry to ask again, but is there any way you can check the footage again? See if at any point it's clear to see if any of them are, well, hiding something, or crawling around on the floor, or something?" she asked, putting her coat back on.

"Sure, I can do that," said William.

"Thanks William. Please, do not discuss this with anyone else and keep your findings in a secured location," said Gillian.

William nodded. "As soon as I have anything, I'll let you know," he said. Gillian smiled at William before grabbing her bag and heading for her office.

CHAPTER TWENTY-THREE
DIGGING IN THE DIRT

New Scotland Yard.25th March - 08:45.

Gillian walked back to her office. She had a feeling inside that the net was closing in on whoever was responsible for the Parliament atrocity. She closed her door, hung up her coat and placed her bag down next to her desk. She sat down and leaned back, thinking. But before she could even begin to think properly, there was a knock at the door. She thought about ignoring it for a change, and hoping whoever it was would go away, but when the knock came again, she conceded.

"Come in," she said.

The door opened and D.S.s Pierce and Cope walked in. "Morning Boss," Mike said. Gillian, looking slightly confused at the pair of them, asked,

"Why are you guys here? Aren't you supposed to be at Parliament?"

"Yeah," said Mike. "But we stopped to get coffees on the way and thought we'd bring you one. You know, on the way. How are you feeling by the way?" Rich placed another cup of coffee on to her desk. Gillian leant back in her chair and crossed her hands, looking at the coffee.

"Oh… I see. Well, thank you. I'm still having real problems sleeping. I think I may see my doctor. Ask to get some blood tests done," she lied. As she said it, she glanced down at her drawers. There was her hair between two pieces of sellotape – and it had broken. Now she knew for sure that she was being watched.

"I don't think you'll need blood tests doing, Boss. It's probably just the stress from this case. Give it a few days, see how you feel," said Mike quickly, looking a little panicked.

"Well, maybe. Anyway, don't let me stop you guys." she said. "Get yourselves off to Parliament. Remember, anything you see or hear which you think is relevant to the case, I need to know first. And thank you for the coffee." Mike and Rich turned and walked out of her office and closed the door behind them.

Gillian sighed. It was becoming harder to avoid them both, and come tomorrow, they would surely know that she wasn't taking her 'medication'. She needed hard facts. She picked up the phone and dialed.

"Hello is that Scotland Yard security? This is D.C..I Harper. Can you tell me if either D.S. Cope or D.S. Pierce entered the building last night after, say 17:00?" she waited.

"I see," she said. "Thank you very much." Gillian hung up the phone and opened her notebook. She wrote '24th March. D.S.s Cope and Pierce re-entered the building at 18:45 and were in the building for only fifteen minutes. My locked desk drawer had been opened again.'

She put her notebook away and picked up the phone again.

"Hello, Records? Yes, this is D.C.I. Harper. I'm after some information which appears to be missing from some suspects' dossiers I have. If I give you the names, can you print me page six of each dossier please?" She read out the names of the sixteen suspects. "Thanks. I'll be down shortly." She hung up the phone. Hopefully, she thought, she might get a clearer picture soon of why someone was hiding information from her.

Scotland Yard – Records Office. 25th March - 09:55.

Gillian arrived at Records. She knocked and entered the room. "Ah, D.C.I. Harper, I have some documents for you," said a lady, and handed her a brown envelope. The office was much smaller than most. There were only four people in this small office space.

"It's strange," said the lady.

"What is?" asked Gillian.

"Well, I remember printing these dossiers out a few days ago for you. I'm sure they all printed correctly."

Gillian shrugged. "Do you remember who you gave the original dossiers to?" Gillian asked.

"Ah yes. It was those lovely D.S.s that work for you. Pierce and Cope, I think?" Gillian, looking down at the envelope in her hands replied, "I guess those pages were just… misplaced. Thanks for printing these again," she said, waving the envelope as she turned. The lady smiled and carried on with her work. Gillian left the office making sure nobody she knew saw her, returning to her own.

New Scotland Yard. 25th March - 10:15.

Gillian entered her office and sat down behind her desk, making sure her door was closed. She placed the envelope she had just retrieved from Records down on her desk, and pulled her chair right up and took a seat. She opened the envelope and pulled the documents out from inside, and there were all the missing page sixes. She began to glance through each one. As suspected, they were previous job histories and immediately she saw the connection. They were all ex-military.

Phillip Marks, Labour, Royal Green Jackets, Major.
Jenny Willow, Labour, Royal Logistics Corps, Captain.
Beverley Carmichael, Labour, Royal Signals, Lieutenant.
Martin Holdsworth, Labour, Paratrooper, Lt. Colonial.
Harvey Scott-Phillips, Labour, Royal Marine, Colonial.
Michael Leighton, Labour, Paratrooper, Captain.
Helen Weston, Conservative, REME, 2nd Lieutenant.
Hakim Sing, Conservative, Royal Logistics Corps, Lieutenant.
Andrew Fallows, Conservative, Coldstream Guards, Major.
Diane McDonald, Conservative, Major Royal Signals, 2nd Lieutenant.
Ben Martin-Walker, Lib Dem, Royal Artillery, Major.
Rachael Powell, Lib Dem, Royal Military Police, Major.
Richard Baker, Conservative, Paratrooper, Lieutenant
William Newton, Green Party, Royal Marines, Sergeant Major.
Joanne Sedgewyck, Green Party, Royal Engineers, Lieutenant.
Matilda Montrose, Independent Party, RAF, Wing Commander.

CHAPTER TWENTY-FOUR
JOINING THE DOTS

New Scotland Yard. 25th March - 10:05.

Gillian sat back in her high-backed, leather chair. She couldn't believe the connection was so simple. They were all in the military. So why hide that from me? she thought. She sat in silence trying to put the pieces together. Pulling out the other files from the drawer she now knew had been compromised, and taking out her small, yellow notebook, she began to think about the connection.

1. Stuart Jones. The suicide bomber. Ex-Paratrooper.

2. Thirty-five M.P.s left the chamber before the explosion.

3. Sixteen of those were ex-military.

4. Sixteen job histories hidden.

5. Sixteen impeccable statements.

6. Any or all of those Sixteen could be suspects.

7. D.S.s Pierce and Cope. Trying to sway the investigation.

8. Blood test report.

Gillian had to have visual confirmation and evidence that explosives were being brought into, and hidden in Parliament. She had to fully rely on William and his team to get that evidence. There was nothing she could do on that front. It was all up to William. So, she decided to do a bit of background digging into both D.S. Pierce and D.S. Cope. Why were they trying to drug her? Why were they trying to sway the investigation?

Gillian had a social media account. She didn't use it very often to post updates, but she used it to keep in touch with relatives and old school friends. She only checked it a couple of times a week, and she didn't even use her real name because she knew there were dozens of people who would love to find her for locking them up. She used her work computer and logged into her social media account. She was already friends with Mike and Rich, both of whom used aliases as well, and she had been linked on social media with them for many years. She searched for them both and went through their update histories and old photos. Family album, drunken nights out, photos of food... and then she found it. A photo album on Mike's social media account labelled 'Army'. She opened the album and there she saw about two dozen photos. Each with Mike in a British Army uniform with Sergeant stripes on his chest. All the photos were taken in different countries with friends or in military vehicles. And he wore a maroon beret, with the badge of the Parachute Regiment. Gillian was amazed. In all the years they'd known each other, he'd never once mentioned his military background.

She then searched for Rich and began going through his photo albums. And again, there, was an older folder marked 'Good Ol'Days' and it held dozens of photographs of Rich in uniform as a Corporal, taken in different countries and again, he wore a maroon beret and badged to the Parachute Regiment. Gillian sat back. "They were all military," she said to herself. She closed her eyes to think.

"Patricia Kaine was due to speak to Parliament on the morning of the 18th with regards to charging Martin Jones, a former Para accused of murder on *Bloody Sunday*. Everyone knew it was going to be a hot topic and it certainly had its critics. Was this case the whole reason for the bomb? Did Stuart Jones hit the nail on the head when he said, '*We've had enough*?' Did he mean veterans? It was a confession, after all. He did walk into Parliament and set off the bomb. And since the Parliament bomb detonation, the entire trial of Martin Jones has been put on hold. There hasn't been a single mention of the trial on the news, because the charge didn't go ahead, and that was because Parliament didn't pass it. And chances are, by the time Parliament is reformed, the charge may even be forgotten.

Gillian opened her eyes. The page sixes. She went through them again. She shuffled the first few pages off, and found the one she was looking for. Richard Baker. Now, Prime Minister. And ex-Paratrooper Lieutenant. "Well what do you know," she whispered to herself. A small smile crept across her face.

CHAPTER TWENTY-FIVE
EVIDENCE INDEED

New Scotland Yard. 25th March - 10:45.

The evidence now seemed to be flowing thick and fast, but Gillian needed the video evidence from William. She knew that was a major piece of evidence and that she'd need it to convince anyone of her theory. The evidence William had provided thus far was compelling, but she needed to see the footage herself. She picked up her desk phone and dialled the short four-digit internal number.

"Hello, William? It's Gillian. Have you managed to come up with anything from the C.C.T.V. yet?" she asked. After a few short moments, she said, "You have? I'll be right down." And with that she hung up the phone. She shuffled all the documents together and put them into her drawer and locked it. Then she left the office and headed toward William's office.

It took a very short amount of time for Gillian to reach William's office. She knocked and went straight in, not waiting for an invitation.

"Ah, Gillian. Welcome. Take a seat." She did, and seemed to be in a hurry about doing it too. William, turning between his screen and Gillian seemed to be on edge, and didn't seem sure about what he wanted to do – either talk to Gillian, or just play the C.C.T.V. footage. Eventually, he decided to press play… and *then* talk.

The footage began.

"What I've done, is I've found a number of… shall we say, questionable clips. I've taken those clips and strung them together in date order. Each clip is only about thirty seconds long but, each thirty second clip seems to distinctly show… well, I'll let you see it and you decide," said William.

Gillian watched. She focused on one spot. Every day, someone different sat in the spot she watched. However, every day, the person sat there, bent forward for a few seconds and disappeared behind the back of the bench. All that was visible on-screen was an arched back and the top of their head. The people sat either side didn't seem concerned. Their focus was on what was happening in the room and were either stood up, shouting or just snoozing. Gillian watched another area. The same happened there. A different M.P. every day, but each day the same. The M.P. sat in the spot, bent down behind the benches. Just for a moment, but long enough. A movement that was just so 'not out of place' unless you were specifically looking for it.

"I see it," said Gillian, shaking her head. "But this evidence is not enough. They could be doing anything behind the bench. Eating a sandwich, tying their shoelaces, anything. They just seem to be bending forwards. We can't see what any of their hands are doing."

William turned to Gillian. "Yes, exactly what I thought" he said, "until I saw… *this*," he said, pointing towards the bottom right corner of the screen. There, over the next few clips Gillian saw it. The camera seemed to be positioned right over one of the six locations and gave a perfect view over the shoulder of the suspects sat there. She watched the clips again. This time focusing on the nearest spot in the bottom right corner of the screen. And there she could see that one by one, M.P.s day after day, leant forward, fumbled around in their bag or case, pulled up a small section of floorboard and then dropped a small white… 'something' into the hole. Each time, the section of floorboard was quickly replaced and a foot placed over it. Each time, the whole process took less than ten seconds.

"We've got them. Holy shit, we've got them." Gillian sat back in her chair, eyes wide, her hands on her head and mouth agape. This was the evidence she needed. Actual video footage of people planting the explosive.

Over the next few minutes, she confirmed with William that the footage he'd collated showed six M.P.s per day leaning forwards and fumbling around. Each day, the nearest location clearly picked up an M.P. placing a square, white package of some kind under the floorboards. She could safely assume that the other five were doing the same thing each day.

"I need this evidence please, William. Do you have a USB stick I can use, please?" she asked. William looked in his bag and pulled out a USB stick. He copied the file onto the stick and handed it to Gillian. She placed it in her bag, again in her large, zip pocket. "Thanks William. Remember, do not talk to anyone about this. Keep it safe."

William smiled. "I will," he said, as Gillian grabbed her belongings and left the office again.

House of Parliament. 25th March - 11:30.

D.S.s Cope and Pierce were sat in their unmarked Vauxhall Vectra, just outside the cordoned-off area of Parliament. It was grey and overcast, with the occasional spit of rain falling onto the windscreen. The pair of them sat in the car, neither speaking. They both had takeout coffee and were intermittently sipping from their cups.

"This is ridiculous," said Mike. "She's got us babysitting other coppers. What was she thinking?" he asked. Rich nodded in agreement.

"Yeah I know. I'm not sure what she's doing either. Maybe it's the weird side effects of that drug we're giving her. Maybe it's causing her to make, I don't know, irrational decisions?" he said.

Mike laughed, almost spitting out a mouthful of coffee. This in turn caused Rich to laugh out loud, a small dribble of coffee dripping onto his tie. After a moment, the laughing died away until there was silence once again.

After a moment, Mike stopped. His eyes grew wide as he stared out through the front windscreen.

"Wait… wait just a minute!" he exclaimed. Rich stopped and looked at Mike.

"What? What's wrong?" he asked.

"Maybe it's not the drugs," said Mike, turning to Rich. "Maybe this… this babysitting job is just to keep us out of the way! What if she knows? What if she suspects?" Mike asked.

Rich stopped for a moment to think. "Nah. She can't do. How could she know? We've got every angle of this case covered. There's *no way* she could suspect… is there?" he asked.

As if both knew what the other was thinking and before either of them spoke again, they put their coffees down into their cup holders and both put their seatbelts on. Mike started the car and the pair sped away, smoke pouring from the wheels as it left.

CHAPTER TWENTY-SIX
THE CLEARING IN THE WOODS

New Scotland Yard. 25th March - 11:35.

The realisation and magnitude of the situation was starting to hit home with Gillian. She'd sat at her desk in peace, going through all of the evidence she had and couldn't see any other angle apart from the one she'd already discovered. This was massive, and possibly went all the way up to the new Prime Minister. Maybe too massive for her. She knew she couldn't trust her Detective Sergeants. The only other way to go was up. So, she decided that the next step was to take her evidence to the Chief Superintendent. She collected together all of the evidence and her laptop. She left the dossiers in her locked drawer, where the D.S.s knew they were. The rest went into her bag.

Gillian put on her coat, picked up her bag and left the building to go for a walk. She needed to get some fresh air and decide in her head, how she would approach the Chief Superintendent with this evidence. She wanted to make sure it was clear, concise and that she wouldn't make a complete hash of it. Any holes in the evidence and the Chief Superintendent would tear her evidence to pieces.

Gillian left Scotland New Yard, looked up at the grey clouds and popped up a small, compact umbrella and walked down the street a short way before turning a corner. As she turned, at the other end of the street, D.S.s Cope and Pierce rounded the corner at high speed in their unmarked car. They pulled their car into the New Scotland Yard car park, and quick as a flash they both exited the vehicle and ran into the building.

Gillian walked until she reached a coffee shop. She checked her purse. Luckily, she had a few pounds in change, and decided to sit and have a coffee. She ordered her cappuccino and took a seat. She sat for some time, just stirring her coffee lost in thought, before remembering to drink it.

Meanwhile, D.S.s Cope and Pierce had obviously found Gillian's office empty. They checked her locked drawer. The documents were still there. "Well, that's something I suppose," said Mike. "But where the hell is she? She must be around here somewhere. You head upstairs Rich, take a look around. I'll head down. We need to know where she is and what she's doing. If she does something unexpected, we're both gonna get it in the neck!"

"Roger that," replied Rich, before they split up to continue their search.

Gillian was the only one who knew everything about this case so far. The D.S.s knew some. William knew some. Susan and Forensics knew some. Her team knew some. Only she knew all of it, and she knew that in order to have this evidence looked into seriously, she would have to tell the Chief Superintendent. The country had suffered a massive loss when Parliament was destroyed. Democracy for a short time was also obliterated. The people of Britain were still in mourning. Gillian could only imagine the carnage this kind of evidence would cause. Could the country handle another major dismantling of Government, so soon after having one destroyed? She knew she couldn't make that call. The only call she *could* make was to the Chief Superintendent, and allow him to make the judgement.

Gillian finished her drink and made her way back to the office from the coffee shop. Her head spinning with details of the case. She made her way into New Scotland Yard and up in the lift to her floor, and walked slowly to the office. She entered and closed the door behind her. Everything seemed to be going in slow motion for her. But, she picked up the phone and dialed the Chief Superintendents number.

"Chief Superintendent Roachford speaking," he stated.

"Sir. This is D.C.I. Harper," she said.

"Yes D.C.I. Harper." He was very short on the phone.

"Sir, I... um... I really need to speak to you. Urgently, about the Parliament case. Could you spare me some time today please?" she asked.

"Ah. Parliament. Yes, big case this. Huge. Of course, D.C.I. Harper. I'm free now until two p.m. if you want?" he said.

"Yes!" Gillian said excitedly. "Sorry – yes, Sir. That would be great," she said.

"Right. Come right up, then." he said, before hanging up. She slowly hung up the phone. There was no backing out now, she thought. She opened her locked drawer and took the dossiers. She put her bag over her shoulder, grabbed her laptop and headed up the two floors to the Chief Superintendent's office.

New Scotland Yard. Chief Superintendent Roachford's office. 25th March - 13:30.

Gillian arrived outside the Chief Superintendent's office. She took a deep breath and raised her hand to knock. Just as she did, Mike rounded the corner and came face to face with Gillian. Shocked, she stopped and faced him. "Mike! What are you doing here?" she asked in a panicky voice. But, just as Mike was about to give his fumbled response, and trying to catch his breath, the door to the Chief Superintendent's office opened. There stood the Chief Superintendent's assistant. It was a basic white painted wooden door with a large, glass panel. The glass was obscured, and had 'Chief Superintendent' written in white lettering on the door. The Chief Superintendent's assistant beckoned Gillian in. "Please, come in. You are expected," she said. She entered. Mike turned around and made his way back downstairs, his face contorted with anger that he didn't catch her in time. He dialled Rich's number on his mobile phone.

"Hi Rich. Yeah, I found her. She's just gone into the Chief Super's office. I know. I'm heading back down now. I don't know what she knows, I didn't get a chance to find out."

The Chief Superintendent sat behind a large, grey, metal desk, with black, leather top. His office was white, with large, wide windows overlooking London. Basic, white blinds covered all the windows. The walls were covered in frames. Awards, certificates, photos of the Chief Superintendent meeting M.P.s and celebrities.

"Yes," he said, as his assistant and Gillian entered the room.

"Sir, I'm D.C.I. Harper," she said.

"Ahhh. D.C.I. Harper," he said, standing up and extending his hand. She shook it.

"Thank you for seeing me at such short notice, Sir," she said.

"Not at all D.C.I. Harper. I've heard a great many good things about you. I'm glad to finally have the chance to chat. Please, take a seat," he said, holding his open hand towards a chair. Gillian sat down as his assistant left the room once more. "So, what have you managed to come up with, in regards to the Parliament case? Interesting one, this one," he said.

Gillian began to explain the facts of the case to him. She made sure she included every bit of evidence. She also expressed her concern regarding her D.S.s, their military past and produced her blood results for the Chief Superintendent to look at and explained how she'd proven that someone was accessing her locked drawers. She explained the C-4, the detonators and the conversation she'd had with the Lieutenant Colonel. The connection between Stuart Jones and the sixteen M.P.s, the suspects' interviews. She even took her laptop out and provided the Chief Superintendent with the C.C.T.V. evidence. Everything.

It took Gillian a good thirty minutes to go through all the evidence and the Chief Superintendent's desk was full of files and paperwork. The Chief Superintendent, who was sat back in his chair, listening intently, slowly sat forward. He brought his hands up to his chin, fingers over his mouth and placed his elbows on the desk in thought, looking down at the evidence.

"D.C.I. Harper, this is excellent work. Strong evidence indeed on all fronts. I can see now why you decided to bring this to me." He sat for a moment, scanning his eyes over the files in thought. Then, quickly he removed his hands and opened his mouth to say something, when there was a knock on his door and the Chief Superintendent's assistant entered.

"Sir," she said, "Your two p.m. is here."

The Chief Superintendent looked at this watch. "Good

Lord, is that the time?" he said. "Right, um, yes. Please hold my two p.m. for just one moment, will you Felicity?" he asked his assistant, holding up his index finger. She closed the door behind her. The Chief Superintendent's face changed back to one of seriousness. "D.C.I. Harper. Do *not* show this evidence to anyone else for now. If what you say is right, then we can't be sure who to trust at this moment in time," he said. "Keep it safe. I will call you soon and we can discuss this further. Excellent work, excellent work. There may even be a promotion on the cards if all of this works out," he said.

Gillian smiled. "Thank you, Sir," she said, standing up and shaking his hand. She collected her documents, put them in her bag and left the room. "Goodbye, Sir," she said as she left. Gillian felt a sense of relief as she walked out. Now she had shared all of the evidence with someone she could trust, someone who clearly showed interest in her findings. She knew then she'd made the right decision and walked with a smile on her face, and almost a skip in her step.

As Gillian returned to her office, she remembered about Mike. She hoped that they weren't on to her. That's the only reason she could think of as to why they were back and why Mike was trying to find her. She got back to her office, opened the door and there were both Rich and Mike, waiting for her.

Gillian, deciding *not* to enter the office and close the door, but instead asked them both straight out from her doorway and rather loudly, making sure that the rest of the office could hear, why there were back and in her office.

"Boss we... um... decided to come back as Forensics on site have found absolutely nothing new and we felt our talents were just being wasted by sitting there," exclaimed Rich.

"Oh, did you now!" shouted Gillian. "The requests and

orders I give aren't good enough for you? You're now giving your own orders? Is that right?"

"Of course not!" said Mike, standing up and pushing Rich out through the door, following quickly behind himself. "Sorry Boss – we'll head straight back there now."

As they left, Mike and Rich talked. "I'm sure now she's on to us. I have no idea why she was in the Chief Super's office, or what she told him. But I think she knows. I don't think we can wait much longer," said Mike.

Rich shook his head. "I don't know. We still don't know if the drugs have taken full effect yet. Maybe she just doesn't know what she's doing," he guessed.

"And maybe she does!" said Mike. "We can't take the risk. She seems too compos-mentis to me. I didn't want to hurt her, but the way she's acting, I don't think we've been left with much choice," he said.

CHAPTER TWENTY-SEVEN
NEVER SWITCH OFF

D.C.I. Harper's home. 25th March - 22:00.

Gillian sat curled up on her sofa with a glass of wine, wearing thick warm pajamas and a pair of woollen, knitted slippers, which had baubles hanging from them. She knew this case was by no means over, but having discussed her findings with the Chief Superintendent, she felt confident that the evidence was there to bring this investigation to a close. In a way, inside she felt a sense of achievement. The television was on, but Gillian sat staring into her glass of wine thinking about the day, when something took hold of her attention. She looked up at the television. The ten o'clock news had just started and the headlines were being read out. What grabbed Gillian's attention was the top story.

"Tonight's news headlines," read the newsreader. "Prime Minister Patricia Kaine's body, which has been lying in state for the past week, will be removed from St. Paul's Cathedral tomorrow morning. She will have a full state funeral on 28th March."

Gillian looked at the television with a confused look. A week already, she thought. How the last week had flown. The last two days also seemed to fly, especially with the absence of D.S.s Pierce and Cope. Their short-term assignment to Parliament had given Gillian the space she needed to perform her own investigation without interruption or subversion. She still had those two to contend with tomorrow, which she wasn't looking forward to.

Despite being relaxed, being a police officer meant she was always 'on duty' as it were. And even though the street on which Gillian lived was fairly busy, she also realised without looking out of the window, that the car that was just passing had been passed three times previously in the last half hour or so – purely by the sound of the engine. It ran slowly. Gillian guessed at maybe ten to fifteen miles per hour. An older diesel. It was noisy and rattled. Possibly a loose exhaust, she thought. Gillian's windows were closed and her blinds were shut and curtains drawn. She couldn't remember anyone in the street in which she lived that had an older diesel with a rattling exhaust. But it wasn't unusual to hear a new car passing. What was unusual was the fact it had been passed numerous times.

Gillian placed her wine on the table, turned off the television and switched off her standard lamp next to the sofa. It was now pitch black in the room apart from the faint glow of an orange street lamp from outside, and as her eyes adjusted to the dark, she slowly turned around, leaned over the back of her sofa, opened the curtains and pulled a single slat of the blind up just a bit. Enough to peek through and see the street. Nothing. The car was gone. No signs of movement in either direction of the street. Gillian sighed and she lowered the slat of the blind. Slowly, she got up from the sofa and turned to make her way to bed. She stopped and turned her head slightly to turn her ear back towards the window. It was the car again.

Gillian now felt very uneasy. At first, she thought she may have been a bit paranoid, but now that the car had passed a fifth time, she knew her intuition was keeping her on the right track. She quickly made her way into her bedroom and changed into some comfortable clothes in case she needed to give chase. She pulled on some tracksuit bottoms and a t-shirt which was lying on a chair near her bedroom door. She also removed the slippers and replaced them with a pair of socks and comfortable trainers.

Finally, she threw on a dark, lightweight hoodie, then made her way back into the living room, turning off her bedroom light behind her.

CHAPTER TWENTY-EIGHT
DIVING FOR COVER

Gillian crept back into her living room. It seemed quiet in the street again and the sound of the car had gone once more. She crept back toward the sofa, and moving the curtains and blinds once more, she took another peek outside. This time, she spotted movement. It was hard to see who or what it was, but she could tell someone was out there. There was movement behind a car on the opposite side of the road. There was movement further up the street, behind a darkened bush. She couldn't make out who it was, she only saw fleeting movement but it was obvious someone was out there, and that they didn't want to be seen.

Gillian moved away from her window again and stood in her darkened living room. She was trying to think quickly what to do. She was contemplating ringing Rich or Mike, and was looking around for her phone. She was slowly turning back towards the sofa when suddenly the window behind her smashed. Shards of glass few in all directions, along with splinters of blinds. Gillian shielded her eyes with her hands and arms, and her flight instincts kicked in. She instantly dropped to the floor for cover. The noise continued. It sounded like a large drum striking the side of the house, again and again. Each time, glass and wood flew across the room in a continuous stream of debris. She could feel plaster and flakes of mortar landing on her hair, her shoulders, her back and on her legs, whilst the banging continued. She fought her animal instinct to scream, and kept her mouth tightly shut as the debris continued to fall all around her and the deafening noise continued. Her heart racing, she knew staying where she was, was a bad idea. She scrambled as low as she could and crawled to another part of the room away from the window. The noise from the window and banging from outside was mixed with the whistles of flying projectiles. She also noticed pieces of picture frames and plaster from her walls were also falling, as she briefly opened her eyes to see what was happening around her. The standard lamp fell and the bulb smashed as the lamp hit the ground near to Gillian. Stuffing began falling having been ejected from inside her sofa. There were fleeting flashes of electricity which lit her room for split seconds as her lamp broke and the television was destroyed. Her ceiling light also seemed to explode. The noise seemed to go on for an age. Gillian's heart pounded, still not absolutely sure what was happening.

Then, the banging stopped as quickly as it had begun. Gillian remained flat on the floor, her ears ringing. She opened her eyes and looked around briefly, and for a few seconds the only noise Gillian could hear in the room was the odd shards of glass falling and the sound of rubble and dust falling onto her hardwood floor. The room settled, the dust began to clear. Her ears still ringing, she scanned the remains of her room.

A thick cloud of brick dust filled the air, which was now glowing orange, reflecting light from the outside streetlight which was making its way through a now very holey pair of shredded curtains and blinds. As Gillian lay motionless on the floor, she noticed shadows moving on the wall. At first, it was the shadows of her blinds and curtains swinging in the breeze through her now-destroyed windows, the shadows cast on the wall by the outside street light. She adjusted her eyes to see it more clearly and at this point she noticed a different shadow. It was definitely the shadow of a person and it was drawing nearer to the house. She slowly sat up, back straight against the wall and tilted her head slightly to look towards the window. There was the sound of a couple of heavy foot falls crunching on broken glass and debris outside her window only a few feet away from where Gillian cowered, but the only part of the person she could see was what appeared to be a long, thin barrel as it began to protrude through the torn and tattered curtains and blinds.

Suddenly she heard shouting in the street. It was one of her neighbours across the road. "Oi! What the hell do you think you're playing at? Don't you know there are kids in bed around here? Bloody playing with fireworks at this time of night! Bloody hooligans!"

The barrel quickly retreated back out through the curtains and blinds, and Gillian heard footsteps run back across her front garden away from the house, as the shouts and screams from the neighbour over the road continued.

As the dust began to clear, Gillian heard the diesel car outside start. It was the same sound, with a rattling exhaust. It revved its engine loudly before a screeching of tyres could be heard and the sound of the car disappeared into the distance.

Gillian remained sitting on the floor for a couple of minutes, waiting to make sure whoever was outside had now gone. She slowly began to get up and brush off the debris from her clothes. The dust from her hair and clothes formed small clouds around her causing her to cough a few times. Gillian, kneeling down, had a quick look outside. The window and blinds were now pretty much non-existent. They seemed to have been blown to pieces. The curtains, now rags, flapped in the breeze from outside. Gillian now had a clear line of sight directly into the street, and apart from the sound of barking dogs, there was nothing. She got up, making sure she wasn't visible from the street and made her way into the kitchen. Uncontrollably shaking, she quickly opened a drawer and withdrew a large, black, metal torch. She tried clicking the button repeatedly until the torch illuminated. Her breathing was now heavy and her adrenaline was spiking through the roof. She slowly moved back towards her living room and shone the torch around. It was then that she realised what had happened for sure.

She grabbed her phone and dialed. "Hello." she panted. "This is D.C.I. Harper. I've just had an attempt on my life. Shots fired. Please send an armed patrol to my home location immediately." She filled them in on her address details and hung up the phone, still hiding around the corner from her living room. Slowly, she peered around into the room again and scanned the room in torchlight. There, on the far wall opposite the window was the evidence she'd feared. Holes. Lots of bullet holes. Looking at the damage it had caused to the window, the blinds and curtains and the room, she estimated that there must have been hundreds of holes, but she was in no mood to start counting them. They had completely smashed her television to pieces. Photos and frames lying in pieces on the floor. The plaster and brick were visible across the entire wall. Not much remained of the original color of the paint.

Gillian slowly sank to the floor, whilst leaning against the wall. The realisation hitting home of what had just happened.

It was clearly an attempt on her life. And the only reason that she could think of, was because of her case. Someone clearly didn't want the real reasons for the bombing at Parliament made public.

As she sat on the floor, she could hear distant sirens slowly getting nearer. The orange dust cloud in her living room was finally settling when Gillian had a sudden thought. She didn't really know who was in on this whole conspiracy. If her D.S.s were in on it, then anybody else could be too. She didn't know who to trust, and with the sirens getting ever closer, she didn't know if the armed officers heading in her direction right now were maybe in on it too.

Gillian started to panic. She looked around frantically looking for her bag containing the evidence. It was next to her sofa, so quickly she grabbed it along with her mobile phone, car keys and a long coat. She then remembered the safe, so made a quick dash to the bedroom office. She tore away the shoes covering her safe, and entered the number. The safe beeped and clicked open. She grabbed the brown envelope and her passport, and leaving the safe door open headed for the door. She wanted to make a quick exit before the armed units arrived. She flung open her door and took a step into the street when she noticed that her car had also taken a hail of bullets. All the windows were smashed, her tyres were flat and steam was rising from the radiator. She wasn't going anywhere in that. She looked around. People from her street were looking through their curtains and stood on their doorsteps, all looking over at Gillian's house having been disturbed by the noise. She looked down the street, and turning the corner into her street a few hundred metres away was an armed response unit, lights flashing and siren blaring. She turned and ran down the side of her house to the back garden, and through a side gate. She ran to the bottom of her garden and scaled a five-foot fence into a neighbour's property. She then ran down the side of their house onto the adjacent street. She quickly dropped her items and put her mac on over her dark clothes. She buttoned it up and tied the belt, before picking up her bag, placing her keys and phone into her pocket just as the sound of screeching tyres came to a stop outside the front of her house. The siren fell silent and she could hear armed officers shouting as they began to advance toward her house. In the distance, she could also see and hear the police helicopter getting nearer, its strong beam of light shining toward the direction of her house from a good couple of miles away. She began to walk quickly up the street to safety, but she didn't have a clue where she was going, or where safety was.

CHAPTER TWENTY-NINE
HUNTED

A park – a few streets away from D.C.I. Harper's home. 25th March - 22:45.

Gillian had taken a seat on a bench in a dark park not too far from her house. The helicopter was still visible, circling the area of her home and hovering occasionally, beaming its strong search light focused straight down on her house, and distant sirens continuing to sound. She knew that as well as armed police, Forensics would now be arriving at her house as well as her D.S.s probably. She knew that involving William or Susan at this point was selfish. She didn't want to drag either of them into this any more than they already were. She thought about ringing her parents, but she didn't know if her calls were being monitored, and the last thing she wanted was to involve them. She checked her phone. No missed calls. She sat, shaking slightly on the bench. She didn't know if it was still the adrenaline or if it was the cold. But she did know that she couldn't stay in the open. She had to stay out of sight and keep a low profile, until the morning at least. Avoiding all other police officers at this point was crucial. She didn't know who she could trust. She walked through the park looking for somewhere to lay low.

As she walked further into the park, she came across a small river running directly through it. There was a small foot bridge crossing the river. She looked around it, and saw a very narrow, concrete ledge underneath the bridge. It didn't look comfy by any means, but it did look dry and secure. Holding onto the side of the bridge, she lowered herself down the bank and onto the ledge. She crawled on her hands and knees under the bridge, and when she was sure she was well under it, she lay on her side, her back to the wall and facing the river. The gap was only about a metre and a half clearance in height but it was enough to hide under. The sound of the river was soothing. It wasn't a constant babble but more of a steady, ripple sound. She lay on her side, staring out across the stream. She curled up into a small ball, and pulled her hood over her head. Lights reflected in the water from white street lights dotted around the park paths. She lay for what seemed like an age before she looked at her watch. 23:07 it read.

Not too long after, she could hear what sounded like the police in the park, as they presumably began to conduct a search for her. There was distant shouting from various voices. They seemed to be shouting at each other across the large distance of the park, and occasionally she heard her name being shouted. She was pretty sure that not all of the police out looking for her were bent, but she knew, that to be sure, she'd have to remain hidden and she'd be safe under the bridge as long as she kept out of sight.

Eventually, the shouting came nearer and nearer, and the light from strong torches were flashing by her on both sides of the bridge. Soon, a number of heavy boots and shoes walked directly over the bridge and the shouting was now directly above her. She huddled in tightly, curling up into the foetal position, making herself as small as possible, and regulating her breathing so she wasn't noisy. As they walked over the bridge, she could hear them talking amongst themselves. Whoever the police officers were, they were discussing her. Between them, they shouted, "We need to extend this line!" "Remember, look for anything!" "We should be out looking for the bastards that tried to kill one of our own!" "Check everywhere!"

Torch lights from above her then scanned the water at either side of the bridge, directly into the water. Gillian stopped breathing altogether, watching, waiting. Torch light then began shining slightly under the bridge and along the water. Eventually, one officer said,

"Nah, nothing here Sergeant." And they began to move on. Gillian lay motionless as the sound of boots eventually left the bridge and the sound of feet crunching on the shingle path disappeared.

Gillian breathed a sigh of relief. She'd been tempted to call out when the officers were near, but knew deep down she couldn't trust any one of them. Not until she could get all of the evidence she carried to safety. As the shouts and calling disappeared into the distance, and the torch lights faded, she crossed her arms and lay with her head on her bag and waited to fall asleep.

CHAPTER THIRTY
WATER UNDER THE BRIDGE

Under the bridge. 26th March - 06:12.

Gillian opened her eyes as the sound of footsteps echoed under the bridge from someone walking their dog over the top of it. For a few seconds she was confused. She didn't know where she was or why she was there. As she scanned the river in front of her, her eyes adjusting to the light, she remembered what had happened. She unfolded her arms and looked at her watch with a squint. As she tried to move, the pain in her body became very apparent. The side she'd slept on was cold. Very cold. And sore. Her neck and shoulders ached and her muscles and joints were unusually stiff. She climbed up onto her hands and knees and slowly moved out from under the bridge once the sound of the dog and its walker disappeared. As she climbed out, she sat up on the bank of the river on a large tree root and stretched. She looked around. It was a grey and overcast morning. There was a thin layer of fog in the park. She watched as the dog walker disappeared into the mist. She guessed the temperature to be around six degrees Celsius, although she felt much colder than that. The mist lay low over the grass and swirled around the trees in the park, and she could see her own breath. There was nobody around and it was eerily quiet.

Gillian rubbed her eyes. She sat on the bank,

contemplating what she was going to do. She checked her bag. Luckily, her purse was in it. She checked it and found about

Twenty pounds in cash and change. She didn't want to use her debit or credit cards because this might give her position away. She slowly stood, stretching as she did, and put her bag over her shoulder. Pulling out her phone, she saw that she had twelve missed calls. All from Mike and Rich. She stared at the phone for a moment, before putting it and everything else back into the bag. She stood and began to walk through the park, her painful muscles and joints easing with every step.

She looked down at herself. Her coat was damp. The knees of her black tracksuit bottoms were slightly muddy. She walked until she reached the far side of the park where she was met by a welcome sight of a petrol station. She looked around before crossing the street. She could see a single man behind the counter in the shop. He was sat reading a newspaper, and there were no customers in the shop and no cars on the forecourt. She left the shelter of the trees and walked across the road towards it, looking in all directions as she did. She entered it. Knowing full well there would be C.C.T.V. surveillance in the station, she kept her head down and her hood up as she entered.

"Morning," she said loudly as she entered. There was a small grunt in response from the man behind the counter, not even looking up from his paper. Gillian wandered around the small shop. There were some warm bacon sandwiches ready and a coffee machine. She poured herself a coffee and took a bacon sandwich to the till. She paid for her breakfast in cash and left the station again, heading back into the park.

She sat and drank her coffee on a bench, watching the odd runner come passed. Every sip was warming and made her feel a whole lot better. With every bite of her bacon sandwich she could feel her energy levels rising. When she'd finished both, she looked at her watch. It was almost 07:30. She had to decide what she was going to do, and with police searches no doubt under way for her, she was running out of time before somebody found her.

Eventually, she decided to ring William once he was in the office. She knew she could trust him. She'd ask him for the Chief Superintendent's phone number and call him directly. So, she sat on her bench and decided to listen to her voicemails as she waited. She had eight voicemails waiting for her. There were four from Rich, each asking her to call him urgently. And four from Mike, explaining what they'd been told and what they'd found at the scene of her house, and pleading for her to get in touch. She deleted all of them. Slowly, the temperature began to rise. The mist cleared and the clouds soon made way for a warming, morning sun. Gillian started to feel better as the rays of sun hit her face.

She looked at her watch. 08:40 it read. She decided to ring William. She dialed and the phone rang.

"Hello," William answered.

"William. It's Gillian." she replied.

"GILLIAN?" he snapped. "Where the hell are you? We've been worried sick!" said William. Gillian interrupted.

"William – I can't talk for long. I'm fine. I can't trust anyone, but I trust you and I need your help. All I need is the Chief Superintendent's number please," she asked.

William, clearly confused asked more questions. "Gillian, everyone is out looking for you! After your call last night, Forensics found your home peppered with bullet holes. We need to call off the search if you're okay!" he said.

153

"WILLIAM! I'm sorry – I just need that number. I can't tell you where I am and *DO NOT* tell anyone I've spoken to you, please! My life is in danger and I cannot trust anyone!" she said again. There was silence for a few seconds.

"Of course," said William. "I'm just worried about you. Everyone is worried about you," he said.

"No, they're not," Gillian replied. "Some are just worried about themselves William."

William read out the Chief Superintendent's phone number. Gillian entered it into her mobile as William read it out. She saved the number, then thanked William for the help.

"I promise you'll be the first to know when I can come back. But for now, just know I'm safe and that I know what I'm doing," she said.

William replied "Look, from what I hear, Forensics believe there were at least three guns involved last night. Best guess at this time is that they were AK-47 automatic rifles. They found around one hundred and forty empty cases on the street outside of your house. Very black-market stuff, not something you can just 'pick up' from a car boot sale. Take care Gillian. Keep your head down." Gillian hung up the phone, then dialed the Chief Superintendent's number.

CHAPTER THIRTY-ONE
LIGHT AT THE END OF THE TUNNEL

Park Bench, London. 26th March - 08:50.

The phone rang a few times. Gillian thought that the Chief Superintendent maybe wasn't in yet. She waited. Eventually the phone was answered.

"Chief Superintendent Roachford speaking," he said. Gillian took a deep breath.

"Sir, it's D.C.I. Harper." she said in a quiet voice.

"My goodness! D.C.I. Harper. Where the hell are you? We've got teams out everywhere looking for you," he said, clearly anxious.

Gillian paused. "Sir, I still have all the evidence. Someone on the inside is trying to eliminate me. I don't know any more who I can trust in the force. That's why I've come directly to you."

The Chief Super thought for a moment. "Gillian. We need to bring you in. You need to keep that evidence safe, and we need you to get it to us – in one piece preferably," he said. "Look – stay out of sight. Spend the day with your head low. Meet me tonight, say nine p.m. I'll give you the postcode of a pub. I'll meet you there. It's a little out of the way, but there shouldn't be anyone there who would recognise us. And it's a well-known busy pub. The Interceptor, I think it's called. There will be lots of public about. Just put the postcode in your maps app and make your way there tonight for nine p.m. I won't tell a soul about this conversation. Got it?" he said.

Gillian was relieved, but confused. "Sir, is there any way of bringing me in today? Or now?" she asked. The Chief Superintendent replied.

"D.C.I. Harper, I have a couple of appointments today. If I cancel those to come and get you, someone in the Yard may get wind that I've 'disappeared' if you know what I mean. You know how rumours go. However, if I stay for the day and leave as per normal, then nobody will be any the wiser. Understand?"

"Yes sir," Gillian replied, "nine p.m.." He gave Gillian the postcode. She took a note of it on her phone. "Thanks Sir. I'll see you tonight," Gillian said.

"Keep safe D.C.I. Harper. We need that evidence," he said.

Gillian hung up the call. She looked up the postcode on her maps app before placing the phone in airplane mode. She did this so that her phone couldn't be tracked. She sat on the bench near the river looking out across the park through the trees and began to plan her route.

CHAPTER THIRTY-TWO
THE LONG WALK

Park Bench, London. 26th March - 09:05.

Gillian had studied the maps app briefly. She'd determined that the rendezvous point was about twelve miles across the city, give or take a few hundred yards, and she had just under twelve hours to get there in one piece. Undetected. Unnoticed. Unseen, and with all evidence intact. She'd studied the map closely. Gathered all the route information and determined which streets were likely to have a bobby on the beat, or likely to have C.C.T.V. active. She didn't want to risk public transport as they all have cameras, as do the majority of taxis and she'd decided the safest way to get across the city was on foot. Although earlier on in the morning, the sun had warmed her nicely after her cold sleep, the clouds had begun to move in and this gave Gillian a perfect excuse to keep her hood raised.

She set off on foot. "twelve miles, twelve hours. That's easily doable," she thought as she set off.

She knew she needed to make herself as inconspicuous as possible. This meant walking, not running. It meant following the rules by waiting at crossings for the green man and crossing the road within a group – not running over the road as an individual. It meant keeping her head down and trying not to raise it too often, when looking at road signs. It meant using her phone as little as possible to save battery. She knew the best way to keep 'off the grid' would be to throw it away completely, but she knew her phone was much more than just a phone. It was her map and only form of communication in case of emergency.

Somewhere in London. 26th March - 11:25.

'Communication.' she thought which stopped her in her tracks. "Exactly!" she said. "Communication! That's exactly what I need to do." She continued on her walk, looking at the shops as she walked. She was looking for a specific type and after a while, she found it.

She stopped right outside and looked around, making sure she wasn't watched before walking in, shoppers brushing passed her as she stood outside. It was an internet café.

Gillian paid cash for fifteen minutes and got to work straight away. The young man behind the counter barely looking up from his mobile phone as he took the cash and gave Gillian her change. Making sure the C.C.T.V. in the store caught nothing but her hooded head, she spent a few minutes scanning all the documents she carried and putting everything she had in digital format, and then put everything she had onto the USB stick in her possession. Then, she sat at one of the more darkened and remote P.C.s in the store and began cramming all the information into a .ZIP file to reduce its size, before emailing all the evidence to two people. The only two people she completely trusted to hold this information. She then added a note.

Hello William and Susan,

I'm sorry to involve you both in all of this, but right now you are the only two people I can completely trust. I've attached a file with all the evidence I have accumulated so far on the Parliament case. I'm trying to avoid contact with any other officers at this moment because I don't know who I can trust. I've spoke to the Chief Super and I think I can trust him. He's asked me to meet him tonight at 21:00 at the Interceptor Pub at postal code TW1 2QJ.

I'm not completely convinced I can trust him yet, which is why I need your help. Can you please make your excuses and attend that location today and set up a camera of some kind on that location? I'm hoping everything will work out well, but just in case anything happens to me then you'll have the video evidence to progress this investigation.

There will be no way for me to contact you after this, and no way for you to contact me either so I'm hoping I get your email addresses correct first time around. Hopefully, I'll be able to buy you both a drink or two after this whole case is put to bed.

Thank you both. I hope to see you soon.
Gillian.

She attached the file labelled 'Kittens.ZIP' so as not to draw too much attention to it by the Met Police I.T. department, and pressed 'send'. A small 'ping' sound was received indicating that the email had been sent, and this put Gillian in a more relaxed temperament straight away. She felt she'd managed to secure the evidence, just in case anything happened to her. She sat for a moment in peace and placed her face in her hands, elbows on the table, rubbing her eyes. Now she was sat down, she felt the fatigue set in.

She looked at her watch. It told her it was 13:40. She opened a map website and found she still had around six miles to go to her rendezvous with the Chief Super. Over seven hours. She knew she'd been making good time, but this was the first time today that she felt fully in control. But, sitting in this internet café wasn't getting her any nearer, so she made sure she'd packed up all of the evidence, removed the USB stick from the P.C. and placed it all back into her bag and closed the zip. She folded her coat and hung it through her bag handles, before correcting her hood and standing up to leave. Waving to the young man behind the counter with a quiet 'thanks' on the way passed, she left the shop and carried on her way.

CHAPTER THIRTY-THREE
RENDEZVOUZ

Pub meeting. 26th March - 20:50.

Gillian had followed the route to the postcode on her phone intermittently throughout the day. She'd traipsed across London on foot, making sure she took a route that wouldn't take her too close to routes normally patrolled by police as they would likely see her, but making sure her route was well-used by members of the public so that she would simply blend in. She spent time in-between resting and keeping her energy up with sandwiches and coffee, occasionally nipping into supermarkets or coffee shops to use the facilities. Gillian followed her maps app on the phone closely. She was glad she was nearly there, because her phone battery was down to three per cent and she was exhausted having covered around twelve miles as the crow flies, but probably more like twenty miles with all the little diversions she took.

It was dusk, almost dark. According to her phone app, she only had a couple of hundred yards to go and the feeling of achievement inside her was enormous. As she rounded what she thought was the final corner, she had an overwhelming sense of thankfulness. Inside, her head was screaming, 'well done,' and her heart was telling her that this case was as good as solved. As she walked towards the spot, she looked up from her phone expecting to see a pub, but all she actually saw was a large, dark, unused, stone-chipped car park. It was flanked on either side by old, tall, run-down and abandoned warehouses. Across the back of the car park, was the edge of the River Thames. As she walked through a set of open temporary gates towards the centre of the car park, her confusion grew. She checked her phone. This was definitely the right place. Her phone was now on one per cent. She turned off the maps and locked the phone. She placed it in her pocket and she walked towards the quayside.

There she stood and looked out across the River Thames, as the last fading shades of orange light of the sun disappeared into the distant west. She turned and looked around again, just in case she'd missed something. But she knew there was nothing she'd missed. She checked her watch. 21:00 it read. She sat on a large, black, cast iron mooring bollard on the quayside and waited.

Something inside her told her something was deeply wrong, but she was tired. She wasn't going to run anymore and she decided to just wait to see what unfolded. Within a few minutes, Gillian heard a car approaching. She sat and watched the road she'd entered on from the far side of the car park. Then, a pair of bright headlights appeared around the corner and a car, driving very slowly, entered the car park. It continued across the car park until it reached the centre and then stopped, headlights shining right at Gillian. The engine then turned off, but the lights remained fixed on Gillian. She tried to shield her eyes a little from the light, as she heard a car door open, but with the headlights pointed right at her she couldn't make out which side of the car had opened. She called out. "Hello? Who's there?" She heard the sound of the car door close, and then slow, steady footsteps walking nearer to her across the stone chips. Standing up, she called out again. "Hello! Who is that?"

This time, there came a response. Just as the dark shadow of a tall man came nearer, it began to block out some of the headlight glare for Gillian.

"D.C.I. Harper – it's Chief Superintendent Roachford," he said.

CHAPTER THIRTY-FOUR
REALISATION

Gillian, blowing a sigh of relief, lowered her arms from shielding her face from the light, and her head dropped in front of her, shaking it slowly in relief.

"Hello Sir. I'll be honest, you scared me for a moment," said Gillian.

Chief Superintendent Roachford approached Gillian and removed his hat, now completely blocking out the light of the headlights.

"Well done for making it here, D.C.I. Harper," he said.

"Where is the pub?" Gillian asked, approaching the Chief Super slightly.

"Well, there is no pub," he said smiling, looking around. "Did you bring the evidence?" he asked.

Gillian nodded. She stood and took her bag off over her head. She opened the bag and showed the Chief Superintendent the contents.

"It's all here Sir." she said.

"Wonderful work, D.C.I. Harper." He took the bag. "I'll take good care of this, D.C.I. Harper. You've done incredibly well. You should feel proud of your achievements over the last week," he said, putting the bag over his shoulder.

"Thank you, Sir. Yes, I do feel proud. But I'll feel better when those responsible are behind bars," she said.

The Chief Superintendent turned around and began to

walk back slowly towards the car, with Gillian walking behind. She stopped in line with the headlights, as the Chief Superintendent opened the boot of the car, and threw the bag inside. Leaving the boot open he turned back to Gillian. He looked down for a few moments at the ground between the two of them, then he placed his hands in his pockets.

"Yes. Proud indeed," he said again. "In fact, we were all impressed," he said quietly.

"*All* impressed?" asked Gillian, confused.

A small smile crept across the Chief Superintendent's face, as his head slowly rose and his eyes stared directly into Gillian's.

"We thought we'd planned the whole thing flawlessly. Crossed the 'T's and dotted the 'I's. We've all been impressed with how you've managed this whole investigation, D.C.I. Harper."

As Gillian tried to make sense of what the Chief Superintendent was saying, the driver's door of the car opened, as did the passenger side door, and out stepped D.S.s Pierce and Cope. They both smiled at Gillian over the open doors. Gillian stared at the Chief Superintendent. She was tired. Her mind was failing to compute what was going on. She couldn't put the pieces together. The look on her face was clear for the Chief Superintendent to read.

"You look confused, D.C.I. Harper. Let me fill you in on a few blanks." he said. "Before I was a Chief Superintendent in the Met, I was Lieutenant Colonel Roachford, of the Parachute Regiment. I served in Northern Ireland as did over three hundred troops under my command. Of those three hundred, ninety-seven died over a three-year period. They died in many ways, D.C.I. Harper. Car bombings. Assassination.

IEDs. Exchange of fire. Ambush. They all had families. Children. Wives. They did their jobs and they did them well. They followed their orders to the letter. My orders.

"My orders were given to me by my Government, D.C.I. Harper." Gillian, stunned, could do nothing more than stand and listen, mouth agape. Her eyes kept flitting between the Chief Superintendent, and the D.S.s who were still stood either side of the car looking directly at Gillian. She didn't know it, but she'd started to break into a cold sweat. Her forehead and upper lip glistened. Her breathing was heavy. Her shoulders and arms slouched by her side in almost total defeat.

"I... I don't understand," said Gillian softly. "You were in on it the whole time?" she asked.

"Yes. In fact, I helped with pretty much everything to do with the organisation of this whole plan." said the Chief Superintendent, a small smile creeping onto one side of his mouth. "I didn't do it all though. Even I needed some help," he said.

He turned to the D.S.s. "These two have done a sterling job. Keeping their eyes on you. Trying to steer your investigation, but they did tell me you were good. And they were right. You're damned good D.C.I. Harper. I certainly underestimated your abilities." Gillian turned to the D.S.s, the car lights still shining. She had to shield her eyes a little to get a good look at the pair of them.

"Mike? Rich? We've worked together for years! Why turn on me now?" she asked. Mike and Rich looked at one another, before Mike spoke.

"Look, Gillian, this was never personal. Whoever had been put on this case, we'd have done the same. I was gutted when we were told you were heading up the investigation.

166

You're a good person Gillian. But this cause that we're fighting for, it's bigger than you. It's bigger than all of us, and sometimes bad things happen to good people. It's called collateral damage. This time, it's you. And I'm sorry for that. I truly am, because I would have liked to have avoided this. You're one of the best D.C.I.s I've ever met, and you too deserve better. Unfortunately, it wasn't meant to be on this occasion. If we had done a better job, or you weren't as damn good as you are, we wouldn't be here. You'd be tucked up in bed at home and our plan would be well under way."

Gillian looking defeated, looked down at the ground in front of her. She slowly sank to her knees. The D.S.s fully emerged from the car, and closed the car doors behind them. The Chief Superintendent walked forwards and stood directly in front of Gillian, hands still in his pockets before slowly lowering himself down and crouching in front of her. He pulled his right hand out of his pocket and with a finger, removed her hood gently, and then moved some hair which had fallen out of place and was waving in front of Gillian's eyes.

"I have the utmost admiration for you D.C.I. Harper, I truly do," said the Chief Superintendent. "And I'm sorry it has come to this." Gillian looked up at the Chief Superintendent, her eyes now filling with tears.

She sniffed. "I really don't understand," she whimpered.

CHAPTER THIRTY-FIVE
CLOSURE

"Let me fill you in on a few more things, shall I?" said the Chief Superintendent. "When there was the first inkling of prosecution for Northern Ireland veterans, a number of us got together to vent our anger and frustration. Veterans now working in all lines of work. Telecommunications, utilities, building, banking and of course, Police and the Government. As time went on and the prospect of prosecution grew, so did our anger. A few members of the Houses of Parliament were amongst those few. All veterans. They tried the best they could with all the legal ways possible to stop this witch-hunt from happening. Petitions, rallies, demonstrations. However, they were heavily outnumbered by pompous and arrogant M.P.s who went to Cambridge or Oxford and who hadn't served a single day in Her Majesty's Forces. When the public heard about it, of course, there was backing for the veterans. But almost full media blackouts of protests and petitions were enforced by the B.B.C. and the like. The Government didn't want the public to have a say on this. That was the final straw."

He stood up and walked around Gillian slowly, stones crunching under his feet, as Gillian remained on her knees looking down at the stones in the car park. "We decided that enough was enough. Many of the M.P.s that helped are still in the Territorial Army, along with a number of others who aren't. After exercises, they were able to smuggle amounts of C-4 from the training areas, with detonators. We collected a hell of a lot of it over the months from a vast number of helpers. The M.P.s who wanted to help, did. By taking the explosive into the Houses of Parliament and hiding it under the wooden seated areas in the Chamber. It didn't take much. A small screwdriver to loosen some floorboards, and making sure that they were in their seats early to ensure they could sit in the right places to deposit the C-4."

Gillian lifted her head. "So, you blew up a homeless man so none of you would have to do the dirty work?" Gillian asked.

The Chief Superintendent continued to walk around Gillian. "We'd also recruited a few more veterans, including Stuart Jones. He'd heard about our meetings from other homeless veterans. He came along and offered his help, especially knowing full well that his brother was one of the veterans on the list to be prosecuted. We knew we'd need a public face. Someone the Police could investigate and point a finger at, someone the public could point their anger towards. We approached him with the idea. He was homeless, his wife and child had left him, he didn't have a job, he had PTSD and he was sick of the world in which we live. He desperately wanted to do it. He desperately wanted to die. We hoped the public confession he made would be enough to put any further police investigations to rest. We obviously didn't count on you being so tenacious."

Gillian, now listening more intently showed signs of calming down. She'd stopped sweating and her breathing had returned to a normal level. She remained kneeling on the gravel carpark, but asked more questions.

"What about the thirty-five M.P.s that walked out. They

weren't all ex-military," said Gillian.

Mike and Rich walked around to the front of the car to join the Chief Superintendent. Mike sat on the bonnet, his arms folded. He sighed before answering Gillian.

"We tried to create a diversion. Yes, we wanted to get our M.P.s out in one piece, but how do you do that without drawing too much attention to them? We tell a handful of other sympathetic M.P.s that a staged walk out of the Chamber as a demonstration to the decision to prosecute veterans will take place. We hoped that our M.P.s mixed in with a group of others with no military past would certainly hinder any kind of strategic investigation."

Gillian spoke up again. "And the drugs in my coffee?" she asked, narrowing her eyes and staring at Mike.

Rich, standing on the other side of Gillian replied. "Look, we like you Gillian. We always have. We didn't want to put you in harm's way. The drugs were just to make you over-tired, in the hope that you wouldn't be able to think straight and maybe have to take some time off, or even drop the investigation altogether and give it to someone else. But, like the Chief Superintendent said, you're too tenacious. We couldn't stop you without, well, bringing about some harm which we really didn't want to do."

Gillian, still kneeling, looked around. There was no running away. No escape without jumping into the Thames.

"So, what now?" she asked. "I completed the investigation. I've found out the truth." The Chief Superintendent smiled.

"Tell me, who else knows as much as you about this investigation, D.C.I. Harper? Who else knows every little detail? Anyone?"

The penny dropped. Suddenly, and only then did she realise. But as far as the Chief Superintendent, Mike and Rich were aware, there was nobody else.

Gillian's tone lowered. "So, that's your plan then, is it? Once I'm out of the way, then what?" Gillian asked.

Mike replied.

"Gillian, we know you're smart. Very smart. You'd pretty much figured out the case on your own, so there was no harm in filling you in on the blanks. But as for telling you what we're planning on doing next?" Mike shook his head. "That is a no-no I'm afraid."

Gillian tried desperately and frantically to think of a way out. Her heart began to race hard in her chest again. She could literally hear and feel the blood pump through her ears. Her breathing rate sped up and she began to sweat again. Slowly she began to stand up, holding her arms out in front of her, holding her hands up to show she wasn't a threat.

"Guys, please. There has to be another way," she said. The Chief Superintendent looked at her, his eyes focusing on her face. Gillian could see on his face that he was thinking. Figuring out what to do next.

He turned to Mike and Rich after a few seconds.

"You know what to do. There can be no strings," he said, and walked to the back of the car. He climbed in and closed the door behind him. Mike and Rich, having watched him get into the car, slowly turned to face one another, before both turned to face Gillian.

"I'm sorry, Gillian. I truly am." said Rich. Mike unbuttoned his suit jacket and reached his right hand around to his back, pulling a pistol into sight. Gillian knew it was now or never. She had no other choice. It was fight or flight.

Quickly, before he could raise the pistol, she kicked Mike in the testicles. He dropped the pistol and fell onto his knees with a resounding, "Oof!" holding onto himself, whilst Gillian made a run for it, barging herself passed Rich, which caused him to lose his balance for a moment. He staggered but regained his balance. Mike shouted, "Get her!" to Rich who left Mike on his knees and ran after Gillian. She was running in trainers, which made it easier, but she still felt like her grip wasn't good running on the stones. She could hear heavy, rapid footsteps behind her, getting closer. She knew she wouldn't make it back to the main road. She wasn't fast enough, so decided to stand and fight.

She slowed, but as she did she pulled her yellow notebook out from her pocket with a pen. She scribbled something on the cover very quickly, then threw the notebook and pen hard, out into the dark carpark. It was very dark now, but Gillian wasn't sure if Rich had seen her throw it. She slowed to a stop and turned around to face him. But Rich was much nearer than she thought he was, and he surprised her. He ran at full speed and like a rugby tackle, wrapped his arms around her, grasped hold of her around her arms and grappled her to the ground. Gillian wriggled and screamed managing to release an arm. With her free hand, she tried to claw at Rich's face. He released Gillian to protect himself, but it was futile. As she scrambled to a sitting position, Rich planted a solid right-hook onto Gillian's cheek. A bright, white flash of light engulfed her vision before she realised she was lying on the stones of the car park once more.

"I'm sorry about that Boss, truly I am," said Rich, as he grabbed her around the waist and picked her up, flinging her over his shoulder. Gillian kicked and screamed.

Rich, out of breath, spoke to her.

"There is no point running Boss. I'm sorry, but there is no other way." He struggled to keep a hold of her as she wriggled frantically, desperately trying to break free. Rich walked her back passed the front of the car and headed towards the edge of the Thames. Just before reaching it, and bending forwards, he threw Gillian off his shoulder onto the gravel in front of the car headlights once more.

Mike stepped forwards.

"Look, if it makes it any easier, we really didn't want to do this. Trust me, I will make sure it's quick and painless." He pulled the hammer back on the pistol and released the safety.

Gillian felt useless. She knew there was nothing she could do. Inside she wanted to fight, to scratch, to bite and to scream, but she knew that whatever she did, she would die tonight. She slowly rose up from her knees and with blood trickling down her chin from her mouth, stood facing Mike and Rich, her shoulders slumped. She took a couple of deep breaths, she lifted her head and closed her eyes.

Everything was black. All she could hear was the rippling of the River Thames behind her and her own solid heartbeat. Then came the inevitable sound she was dreading.

BANG!

CHAPTER THIRTY-SIX
AFTERMATH

Gillian's murder scene. 26th March - 21:35.

William Hacket and Susan Pritchard emerged from a darkened building adjacent to the car park. They walked silently into the car park through the temporary gates. They'd just witnessed what happened and watched, as Gillian's body had been thrown into the Thames. They watched as Rich and Mike had both returned to the car with the Chief Superintendent in the back, and turned the car around before quietly exiting the car park and pulling away.

William and Susan waited a good few minutes before leaving the safety of the darkened building, just to make sure that nobody was coming back before making their way across the road. They reached the far side of the car park and looked over the edge into the dark waters of the Thames. There was no sign of Gillian. Susan held a hand over her mouth, trying to stifle her crying but she wasn't doing a very good job. She staggered backwards slowly, holding out a hand behind her trying to find the cast iron mooring bollard that Gillian had sat on earlier in the evening to steady herself, and eventually sat down onto it. William just stood on the edge of the quayside looking down into the darkened waters, his hands in his pockets. Neither of them spoke for a good few moments. It wasn't until Susan let out another small whimper that William snapped out of his daze, stood bolt upright and turned to face her.

"Right. We need to get the portable camera. Now! I'll take the camera and the footage and make sure it gets to New Scotland Yard first thing tomorrow morning. Susan, you need to get home. Have a drink or two. Or even three. Have a bath and try to get some sleep. You were never here, got it?"

Susan, still clearly shaken, just stared into the waters. Her hand still across her mouth and her whole body was physically shaking.

"Susan! Did you hear me?" said William, in a more raised but yet still whispered tone.

Shocked, Susan turned to look at William. The pure terror in her eyes was plain to see. This had shocked her to the core.

"Um, yes. Yes, I heard you," she said softly in reply.

William put his hands in his pockets and turned to return to the darkened building. "Come on Susan. We need to make sure the footage captured everything," said William, gesturing the direction they needed to go with his head. Susan stood up to follow him. They silently made their way back to the building through the temporary gates and across the street. The building was what appeared to be an abandoned warehouse. As they entered through an old, rusty, metal doorway on the ground floor, William turned on a torch which he had in his pocket. It lit up the floor immediately before them. Susan followed in behind, watching her steps and matching her feet falls to those of William's before her. The room was large and open. It was obvious that the building hadn't been in use for some time. There was barely any plaster on the walls. The ceiling was mostly open and rotten, wooden beams. The floor was littered with bricks, dust and rubble, and every foot fall was greeted with a creaking of old floorboards. As they reached the far side of the room, they began to climb the old, rickety, wooden stairs they had climbed earlier to set up the camera equipment located on the first floor. It was obvious nobody else had been there in many months, if not years, as there were only two sets of prints in the dust around them and on the stairs, and they belonged to both William and Susan. They reached the first floor and made their way to the front of the building, and to a window, which was open to the elements. It had a rotten, wooden frame with the odd fleck of white paint still visible, but no glass remained in it. It was clearly once a grand window which was probably used by a rich import business owner to overlook a busy port and watch his ships come and go.

William kneeled down. On the wooden floor next to the window was an open laptop. It was showing a view from the camera at the window. Connected to it, was a long cable which stretched up the wall to the window and there sat on the window sill was the camera. William pressed a few buttons on the laptop which stopped the recording. He turned off the camera and pulled it down from the windowsill and he handed it to Susan. "Here, can you wrap up the cable and put it away in the bag please?" he asked, trying to keep her busy. She took the camera and did her best to wrap the cable away, visibly shaking as she did so.

Whilst Susan did that, he checked the recording files. He clicked into the hard drive where the files were kept and opened one. The video began to play. He skipped on a short while before pressing play again. The image was clear and crisp. The camera's night vision had captured everything perfectly, including the number plate of the car, and each and every face that had appeared tonight. There was no mistaking who was there, or what had happened. William stopped the recording and closed the laptop. He placed it into a large, black bag. Susan handed him the camera in a small, black bag and he placed that into the laptop bag also. He zipped it up and flung it over his shoulder as he stood up.

William turned to Susan. "Are you okay?" he asked. Susan just looked at him. Her eyes filled with tears. She shook her head before covering her mouth with a hand again and screwed her eyes up tight. William leant into her and hugged her tightly. She gripped him back, clawing at loose material on the back of his jacket.

"Okay, I'll take you home and make sure you get there safe. Come on," he said, as he guided her back towards the staircase with one arm over her shoulder and the other guiding the way with the torch.

They both walked through a couple of quiet streets before making it back to William's car. The sound of distant sirens and trains could still be heard from a city that never sleeps. He unlocked it and placed the bag into the boot. It was an older car. A mid-eighties Ford Escort but in beautiful condition. William clearly looked after it very well. He then went around to the passenger side and opened the door for Susan. As she lowered herself into the car, William scanned the street around him making sure nobody saw them. Once inside, he gently closed the passenger door and proceeded to walk around to the driver's side. He climbed inside, turned on the lights and the car pulled away.

CHAPTER THIRTY-SEVEN
OVER AND OUT

New Scotland Yard. 27th March - 14:30.

William Hacket sat at his desk. He was staring at his computer screen, scrutinising footage closely. It was the footage they'd captured the night before. Using his mouse and controls, he was freezing frames of footage, then rewinding, then freezing again, then forwarding again. He hadn't left his desk all day. It was strewn with empty sandwich cartons, empty cardboard coffee cups, paperwork and photographs. His bin overflowed with the same and looked like it hadn't been emptied for days, even though it had been the day before. On the wall behind him was a flat screen television and the channel it was on was Sky News. The volume was low, but just high enough for background noise.

William sat back in his chair, having been staring at the screen for many hours. He removed his glasses with one hand and rubbed his eyes with his other. His eyes ached, which wasn't unusual but on this occasion, it was mostly due to being up late and a lack of sleep. He sat with his eyes closed for a few moments trying to give them a short rest.

He listened to the television. Although it was set on a low volume, he could just hear it. And it was because he could just about hear it, he opened his eyes and swung his chair around to watch it for a few moments. He checked his desk for the remote. He cleared a few photographs and sheets of paper in his hunt, finally finding it on the floor by his desk and returning his glasses to his face, he turned the volume up so he could hear it properly.

"And the main headlines again today. Former Prime Minister Patricia Kaine's body was removed from St. Paul's Cathedral yesterday. The streets were lined with over one hundred thousand mourners, all hoping to catch one last glimpse of the coffin before it was taken away in preparation for her state funeral, which will be carried out next week, details of which are yet to be released. She has been lying in state for one week."

"Prime Minister Richard Baker paid tribute to Patricia Kaine from No.10 Downing Street today. This came just after he had officially unveiled his new Cabinet of Ministers to the press and public, in an official 10 Downing Street press release. Also released, was an official statement confirming that Patricia Kaine's campaign against Bloody Sunday veterans will *not* be taken any further. An official statement from Sinn Fein in response was released earlier today, which stated that they were disappointed with the decision." William watched the news with interest. His face straight.

"The Metropolitan Police today confirmed that the bombing of Parliament was carried out by Stewart Jones. The police confirm that C.C.T.V. footage recovered from Parliament *does* place Stuart at the scene at the time of the bombing. His confession released to the press a number of days after the incident had been officially submitted as evidence following the confirmation from police that he was the individual who triggered the bomb. The police are not looking for anyone else in connection with the incident.

179

"The body of a woman has been found in the Thames this morning by a dog walker. It hasn't been officially confirmed but police suspect this may be the body of Gillian Harper, a Metropolitan Police Detective Chief Inspector who disappeared two days ago. Police divers are also on the scene dredging a section of river for what is thought to be a weapon. At this stage, the police are treating her death as suicide. Chief Superintendent Roachford paid respects to Gillian this afternoon." The television cut to a scene of Scotland Yard and Chief Superintendent Roachford stood outside, dressed in his best uniform.

"It is with great regret that we believe the body of a woman, thought to be Detective Chief Inspector Harper has been found in the Thames this morning. Her body was discovered by a dog walker at around 07:30. Initial investigations believe she died from a single, self-inflicted gunshot wound to the head. She had recently been suffering with mental illness and depression. All of our thoughts here at the Metropolitan Police are with Gillian's family at this sad time."

William lowered his head. He sat back in his chair and stared at the floor for a few moments. He turned his chair back towards his desk slowly, the news reader continuing to read the news headlines. He opened a drawer in his desk and pulled out a small brown envelope. On it was written 'D.C.I. Harper – Parliament.'

He opened the envelope and tipped it slightly. Out fell a plain, black USB stick. This was a copy of all the evidence Gillian had emailed him the day before. It contained all the C.C.T.V. evidence he'd given to Gillian, plus the information relating to the sitting positions of the M.P.s and the locality of the explosives and the missing page six documents from the statements. He put the USB stick into a USB port in his P.C. and the documents back in the envelope, and placed that back in his drawer.

As he sat thinking, a Police Constable knocked on his office door and entered the room. "Hello William," he said.

"Ah, P.C. Horner. How can I help?" William asked slightly confused.

The constable approached William. He placed his hand in his pocket and, looking around, took out a clear, plastic evidence bag which was sealed. It contained what appeared to be a notebook. The constable looked at it for a moment, before handing it over to William. "I was part of the team on the ground this morning after D.C.I. Gillian Harper's body was found. Whilst we were carrying out an area search, I found this not too far from where she was discovered."

William took the evidence bag from the constable and looked at it. He looked up at the P.C. before opening it and slipped the notebook out. He instantly recognised it as Gillian's notebook. It was a plain notebook, yellow in colour but on the front was scribbled 'W. Hacket'. He looked back at the P.C. with a confused look.

"I decided not to take a note of this find, so nobody knows about it. I flicked through it, it's full of names and notes but I can't make head nor tail of them. I thought I'd better hand it straight to you," said P.C. Horner.

William, still holding the book, looked at it again. "Thank you," said William. The P.C. smiled and left the room.

William turned back towards his desk and leaning forward with his elbows on his desk, began to flick through the pages of the notebook. He spent a few seconds reading through sections of it.

"And finally," said the news reporter on the television, "the family of a missing lady are appealing for any information in helping to find her after she went missing yesterday afternoon. Susan Pritchard has not been seen since around two p.m. yesterday afternoon."

The T.V. showed a photograph of Susan smiling. "Anyone with any information about the whereabouts of Susan are urged to contact police immediately."

William looked up from his computer and smiled. He turned and rolled his chair towards a shredder nearby. He immediately fed Gillian's yellow notebook into it. The shredder tore through it with ease and in seconds. He then took the brown envelope from his drawer and did the same with that.

Turning back to his computer, he opened a window on the screen from the USB drive. He clicked the mouse which produced a menu on the screen and he moved the mouse over the word 'Format' before clicking it. Suddenly, the USB stick was blank. Empty. Everything deleted. He pulled it out from the computer and threw it into his drawer. The same drawer he'd initially taken it out of to give to Gillian many days before.

William sat back in his chair and rolled up his sleeves, smiling the whole time. On his right forearm was a tattoo. It was old and faded, but it was clear for all to see what it was.

Pegasus rising.

The End.

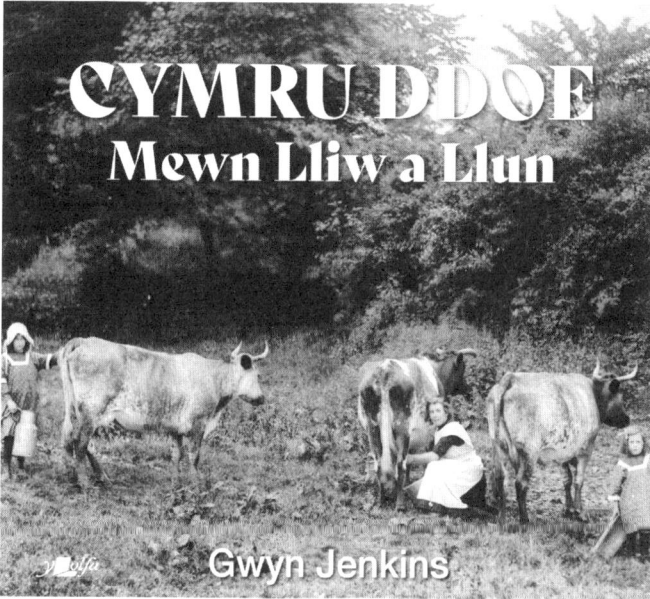

CYMRU DDOE
Mewn Lliw a Llun

Gwyn Jenkins

£19.99
(cc)